THISTLE

THISTLE NADIA DE VRIES

TRANSLATED BY SARAH TIMMER HARVEY

the New Menard Press

I want to run away into the woods;
to kill weasels in wheat silos;
to live in the woods,
with my disfigured face exposed,
without a name;
to stay in the woods until I belong to the woods—
and if somebody finds me alive,
and they may,
they'll shoot.

—Selima Hill, 'I Want to Run Away'

It was morning, and I was listening to pop music for lonely people. My body felt like a glove on the bathroom floor – or like someone else's glove, because it didn't fit me.

The drain still stank. The scent of human flesh, once smelt, is unforgettable. The green light on my phone told me I was dangerous.

I heard an unfamiliar voice in my head. It said that an animal had devoured another animal. And that I would grow very old.

My body has always belonged to me. In the past, I was pure and clean and had nothing to fear. Police officers, judges and teachers were more frightened of me than I was of them.

Behind the curtain, the world was waving at me, and she seemed very kind.

A SELF-PORTRAIT

It was either overdue maintenance or turbulence that caused the accident. Our lawyer argued for the former and the airline's lawyer for the latter. The airline's lawyer was more expensive than ours, and the judge ruled in his favour. That day, the compensation for our grief was a settlement payout and five ceramic pelicans bearing the airline's logo, which were popular collector's items. The three of us were each supposed to get our own set of pelicans, the representative promised, but the money went solely to our mother. After the hearing, we had a house with fifteen ceramic pelicans and no father.

My Sister, who was six years older than me, smashed her set to pieces. I kept mine.

At the funeral – purely ceremonial because there wasn't an actual body – we served marzipan petit fours because they had been my father's favourite cake. Whenever he was home on a Saturday, he liked to eat them with his morning coffee to protest against 'healthy' breakfasts.

He wanted to show us how to enjoy the mundane things in life, all the little freedoms that humans could permit themselves.

That morning, we'd picked up one hundred and fifty marzipan petit fours, because that's how many people we expected at the funeral. Sister and I had taken a taxi to the patisserie, and when the girl behind the counter asked us if we were heading to a big party, we said: No, we're in mourning.

For years, I believed that marzipan petit fours gave me diarrhoea because I was so upset about my dead father. And it wasn't just the petit fours; ice cream, milkshakes, and butter cakes also sent me running for the toilet. I thought a grieving body couldn't handle anything sweet, until I turned vegan when I was twenty-five and discovered that it had absolutely nothing to do with grief. It was the dairy – I'd been lactose intolerant all that time.

The body, I learned, is full of secrets.

The funeral service began at noon. By then, the marzipan fondant on the petit fours had already gone soft. It was the last week in May, and the days no longer felt refrigerated. If a body had been in the coffin, it would have to be kept extra cool to prevent it from smelling. But that day, there was no body to bury, just a name and an idea. We were crying at the mere suggestion of him. The funeral was for us – my mother, Sister, and I – specifically for our grieving process, so we'd still get to experience a 'normal' funeral despite the bizarre circumstances surrounding my father's death. We'd missed out on all the other parts of a 'normal' funeral, like caring for and laying out his body. My father had nothing to gain from the burial; he'd been burnt alive, or pieces of his flesh were bobbing around somewhere in the Atlantic Ocean. Both options were impossible for us to imagine, so we were grateful for the coffin, which gave the impression that there was still something peaceful about the whole situation. Essentially, the funeral service was nothing more than an eight-thousand-euro therapy session. But our peace of mind was entirely worth that sum of money.

A classmate's mother had invited me to make a bracelet the previous Monday. The mother gave workshops and was a professional artist. She said I might find it comforting to give my father something. I didn't dare tell her that there was nothing I could give, but I accepted her offer of a crafting session and wove a bracelet out of the colours I most liked to wear (purple, pink and yellow). Sister said I should put the bracelet in the coffin, but I refused, wanting to keep the bracelet for myself so the whole grieving circus would leave me with at least one nice thing, but according to my Sister, this was unacceptable. We got into an intense argument, and by the end, we'd managed to break the bracelet apart. I shrieked that it was all so unfair. *You'd better get used to it*, my mother called up the stairs.

The sky was very blue. I remember it being the perfect day for a soft-drink commercial, and the taxi driver's phone constantly ringing. His ringtone was *The Godfather* theme song. The first time his phone rang, it felt vaguely tragic, but I could barely contain my laughter by the third phone call. Sister almost slapped the driver's face, but sadly, we had a funeral to attend and couldn't be late. We had duties to perform.

I remember feeling very old in that moment.

The coffin was made from bamboo because that was better for the environment. The airline paid for the coffin. I wore new shoes, black pumps with chunky, square heels and ugly grooves in the soles. Gravel from the driveway kept getting stuck in them. Sensible shoes would be out of the question at my funeral. And instead of a bamboo coffin, I wanted a linen shroud so my body would burn quickly. And I wouldn't have any children weeping over petit fours because I wanted to save them from that kind of suffering. No, none of my children would ever become orphans because they wouldn't be born in the first place.

We'd chosen a song by David Bowie. One of the employees at the funeral home had accidentally downloaded the live version, and when the song ended, we heard thunderous applause from an invisible audience. One of my father's childhood friends, whom I'd never met, read a poem by Lucebert. My mother and I lit candles; her brother, our uncle, played something on his guitar. Finally, Sister gave a speech about her new tattoo, which she'd gotten as a tribute to our father. It was a red admiral butterfly on her right shoulder. She warned us that it still wasn't fully healed before revealing it at the end of her speech. Vague acquaintances wept.

Oh no, not me. I never lost control.

A weasel crept out from behind the curtain that obscured our view of the graveyard. It stole along the podium, past the pulpit, right by Sister as she spoke about her tattoo, and bore its tiny teeth. He was an ugly animal with a disproportionately long neck, which was practically begging to be strangled. But I was the only one who noticed him.

Now that I think about it, it was a beautiful day. We weren't in recession or at war. The flowers at the graveyard smelt very sweet. The bees must have gone wild and gorged themselves. Yes, it was a particularly gorgeous day, at least for the rest of the world.

After the ceremony, my mother clawed the bamboo coffin. Don't leave, she said, stay a while, just a little while, you can't go now! Everyone knew the coffin was empty, and the people who didn't know us very well gripped my Sister and me and repeated: It'll be okay, it'll be okay. My mother was given a glass of wine.

She skipped the marzipan petit fours, and once the wine hit her bloodstream, she started laughing louder and louder. And this was how my mother had been dealing with discomfort since my father disappeared: by laughing very loudly.

We'd explicitly stated on the funeral invitation that we didn't want any flowers, but no one seemed to have paid any attention to our request. The reception room was filled with bouquets. My mother, who'd gotten very drunk in the meantime, suggested throwing the flowers into the grave so that 'at least something would decompose in that hole', but Sister and I felt that would be ungrateful. We placed half of the floral arrangements around the grave's edge and took the rest home with us. We barely managed to fit the flowers in the boot of the car, and my mother had to laugh at that, too. Our house looked like the dressing room of a famous actress for an entire week. Then, the flowers began to stink, and we had to throw them in the compost bin in the back garden.

I feel like my childhood was long and drawn-out, but I can't remember any of it. I do recall spool knitting sets, French castles and loads of stupid little songs, but the lack of inhibition that children have, I don't remember that at all. And I don't talk about my childhood in a tone that suggests it was a blissful time, like some kind of holy fever dream, but then without the fever. I have literally no ties with the past. In my mind, I bit holes in every bouncy castle until it deflated. I am silent whenever someone announces their pregnancy. And in the month of December, I keep to myself.

One of my mother's friends recommended we see a therapist. The woman in question was specialised in bereavement counselling and practised at her home. My mother decided to give it a try, which automatically meant that Sister and I also had to try it. We went on a Thursday during my exam week, just after I'd taken my final exam of the year. It had been a maths exam, and I'd eventually get an A minus for it, but I would only hear that a few weeks later.

The therapist smiled with her mouth closed when she opened the door. We had to walk through her living room to get to her practice space. She had a teenage son who was around my age. He was gaming on the television when we stepped inside, playing a first-person shooter in a war-themed game. I watched a Nazi soldier's body explode onscreen. His death was worth fifty points. *Ughhh*, said his wounded comrade, just before the teenage son got him in the head, and the character disappeared from the screen.

A decade later, on dating apps, I'd come across loads of young men who used their hands to mimic a gun in their profile picture. Some pointed their fingers at the camera, others aimed at their own heads, but in their bios, both kinds of men would claim they weren't looking for any 'crazy chicks'. Where did they get the self-confidence to express a preference? These guys belonged on a police watchlist or in a closed room with no sharp edges or shoelaces. Despite this, they were looking for love.

Coffee or tea? the bereavement therapist asked, and my Sister and I both said: Water. I don't remember what my mother had to drink.

In the practice room, there was a table with a bowl of potpourri on it. A silkscreen print of an apple was hanging on one of the walls, while Monet's waterlilies decorated another wall. Luckily, we didn't have to talk about ourselves. Instead, we played a ball game, though the 'ball' looked more like a beanbag. We were supposed to toss the beanbag to each other while saying random words that would reveal our deepest needs. The therapist didn't participate; she was the referee. My random words were *gag*, *bond* and *vicious*.

At the end of the session, everything felt artificial – my voice, my shoes, the way I said goodbye – and according to my mother, this meant the therapy had worked. We celebrated our victory in a sushi restaurant, where Sister had a panic attack because of the dried bonito flakes in her soup. Those flakes are taunting us, she cried. They're mocking us because Papa is dead, and we're just getting on with our lives. My mother immediately started laughing loudly again, which prompted Sister to put on her jacket and tell us that she never wanted to see us again.

She was exaggerating, but things would never return to how they once were. Sister withdrew from her philosophy degree and went to study law in another city, in a different community. She moved into a sorority house. The other girls in her house made her swim naked through a canal before she was allowed to move her things into her room. I didn't hear this directly from Sister. I ended up reading it in the paper. The reporter said it had made the regional news because the incident was so incredibly humiliating. But when I heard the news, I thought primarily about the butterfly and the risk of infection from swimming through canals with an open wound and those horrible sorority arseholes who didn't understand the meaning of the tattoo.

Ughhh, said the voice in my head.

I'd just finished my first year of high school and was waiting for my first period to arrive. My mother got herself a comfort dog, which would occasionally be in heat. My mother wouldn't have it sterilised because she thought that would be sad for the dog. She didn't believe in dog nappies either. For as long as I still lived at home, twice a year, I'd find myself stepping in the blood of a bitch in heat. And I'd have to tolerate my mother's lovers.

The weasel I had seen at the funeral continued to visit me. Occasionally, I'd find him in my bedroom, usually after school when I was tired. I could never summon or influence him; he would visit when it suited him. And while his visits were unpredictable, it seemed like the animal felt at home with me. He even brought some friends with him one day. The five of them crept over my clothes, books, and bed. They sang pop songs and bit my Barbie dolls' feet, making it look like they had toes. Once the weasels had gone, I wrapped my dolls in newspaper – battered, worthless – and threw them in the bin. When my mother asked what was inside the mysterious packages, I told her they were filled with bloody tampons.

Gradually, we forgot my father's shoe size.

By the time I reached upper secondary school, my average grade was no longer an A. I got Cs for my final exams and didn't apply for college or university studies. I was far from ambitious, but my mother was nevertheless very proud of her girl. She wanted to buy me a present to celebrate my graduation. It could be whatever I wanted, large or small. I chose a digital camera that I'd seen in a music video. In the video, all the girls who'd initially been lurking in the shadows began dancing sexily as soon as the camera appeared. It was utterly irresistible and made me realise I also wanted to be the girl in the spotlight.

I was seventeen, lonely and angry. Afraid I'd lost my teenage years to grief and other darkness. Before too long, I would lose my girlish body to stretchmarks and violin hips. All the smoothness would be worn out of me and eventually replaced by something unknown, and I wasn't ready for that. I wanted to hold onto my teenage body – and the personality attached to it – for as long as I could. I didn't want to set foot in a voting booth, pay a premium or own a boiler. I wanted to wear chipped nail polish and invent my own dance moves. I wanted to be young and reckless and wild. The future, with all her ugly obligations, must be delayed as long as possible.

When you grow up, you'll need to find a good man, said my mother, *so you won't have to work a day in your life.*

The light in my bedroom was bright. I took off my clothes. The button on my jeans had left a print on my skin, and from a distance, it looked like I was suffering from atopic dermatitis. I stood in front of the mirror, clutching my camera in one hand. My thumb was only just flexible enough to reach the shutter release.

I wasn't naturally talented and didn't possess the hand-eye coordination necessary to look in the mirror while also keeping myself in front of the lens. It was only by pulling the most unflattering facial expressions that I managed to take a clear picture. I took a photo but wasn't satisfied with it, so I took another one. Then another. I wanted to be sultry, but I wasn't anything like the girls in the video. Nothing about me was sensual or free.

Soon, I would turn eighteen.

I linked the camera to the computer with the cable that came with it. I needed to see myself onscreen, to admire myself through someone else's eyes. The size of the file reflected how much space my body occupied. I was smaller than I'd initially thought, which comforted me.

There were photos in which I looked very focused, and pictures of me pouting, pictures of me feigning horniness by grabbing my left breast. I was the embodiment of every woman I'd ever seen on television. All the while, the weasel watched me – and his friends were watching, too. The largest weasel, their leader, bared his teeth and sneered. *If you want to be a show pony, you must first become a workhorse*, he preached in the language of lesser beings.

His criticism left me cold. I saved all the photos in a new folder and copied that onto my external hard drive, which I'd named The Black Box, to mark the occasion. That box was the part of myself that others could only access once I'd been completely smashed to smithereens.

That evening, I learned that I was worthy of being a picture. I was proud of my body and of how porous and multifaceted it was. My body impressed me with the secrets it held. I was terrified of the possibilities it comprised and exhausted by the fantasies I'd created for it that drifted further away from reality the older I got.

I disconnected the Black Box from my computer, put it on top of a pile of magazines, and returned to my teenaged existence, with its dog blood and wild animals.

And I completely forgot about the photos.

The five pelicans now inhabit the windowsill in my kitchen, and there's something small hidden inside one of them. I'm not exactly sure what it is, but when I pick up the figurine and shake it, something rattles inside. The other four pelicans are perfectly flawless and hollow; nothing is rattling around inside of them. I could break open the offending pelican to find out what's inside, but that would be cruel, like laughing at an animal that's in pain or dying – or laughing at an animal acting strangely because it's in pain or dying.

Do you remember? When you still had a child's body, but your thoughts were already adult?

SOME THIRTY-SOMETHINGS GET WRINKLES FROM LAUGHTER, BUT I'M NOT ONE OF THEM.

I am an adult now, something I've only recently learned. It happened the day my father had been dead for exactly twenty years. I was walking through the park, enjoying the moment. It was spring, and the days were long. No one was harmed by the implementation of my ideas. A shoeless man asked me if I could spare some change.

There was a fountain by the park entrance. A mother had parked her stroller beside it, and the child sat inside admiring the water. The mother pointed at the streams of water that shot out of the ground in an unknown rhythm. It was endlessly delightful, hearing their little noises. The child was dressed in neutral colours, but I could tell it was a little girl.

My photography teacher taught me to be always at the ready. In a city like this, you can find magic in the streets.

I'd bought a bag made of faux crocodile skin for my camera. It was always on my shoulder. You can never be sure when the magic will happen, and if you don't have your camera, you're just a bystander.

Crouching just behind the stroller, I assumed the position of observer. A woman in her thirties wearing nice shoes will always be considered harmless. I could do whatever I wanted, and I took advantage of that. I held my camera, ready to spring to action when the scene struck the right balance between beauty and discomfort.

The stones surrounding the fountain were slippery. It was a perfect storm in the making. A wet surface and a small child don't always go well together. The mother had no idea what was happening. She didn't even hear my camera's shutter clicking. I was secretly making her child mine, planning to frame her picture and put it on my desk at home.

This is how my transformation began. Behind the lens, I became a nasty creature with a foul aura. The light, which had been decidedly spring-like, suddenly felt grim and menacing. The parakeets in the trees stopped screeching. The fences around the park, the shrubbery, and the water in the fountain all suddenly appeared to be made of human flesh and smelled like it, too. The world was like a stranger's unwashed body.

Are you all right, Madam? asked the mother.

Time was lost. The mother now stood beside me, but I hadn't seen her move. I had to hide the camera, appear harmless, and de-escalate. I wanted to give a positive answer to the question she had asked, but before I could regain control of my mouth, I felt an old familiar warmth in my crotch. While squatting behind the stroller, with my camera in hand, I'd pissed in my pants.

I had to sing a song for one of my assessments during my first year of high school. My performance was appalling, and all my classmates were there to see it. The song I chose was far beyond my capabilities, and there was a long instrumental interlude halfway through it, during which I could have danced if I hadn't been so frightened. That memory came to me as I was sitting on the ground, trying to find an anchor for my shame.

Yes, I said to the mother, Yesyesyesyesyes.

I used the fake crocodile to cover myself, switching between my backside and my crotch, depending on which side other people were passing me by. *Right, left, right!* I must have looked so nervous. To limit my humiliation, I chose to take the path through the bushes to get home. While en route, I stepped on a condom and two human shits, neither of which was fresh enough to stick to my shoes.

The branches hung low. I had to keep my body bent while walking, or they would slap me in the face. Every so often, a leaf would tickle my back, and I'd know I wasn't close enough to the ground.

A tick jumped from one of the branches onto my collar. The insect had mistaken my fur coat for an animal. Oh, he was so wrong! My fur was synthetic and detachable, so the tick would stay hungry.

I crept out of the bushes and thought about the mother, who had called me 'Madam'. She'd assumed I was too old for casual language. In her eyes, I was a real woman, perhaps even a lady, whereas her child hadn't even noticed me. Later, when the girl was old enough to play outside without supervision, her mother would remind her of me. I would be her example of why you can't always trust strangers. It can happen in the blink of an eye, this transformation, relegated from human to teachable moment.

The tick crept from my collar to my neck, and I asked him, *Why?*

GRIEF IS A PARASITE

The next day, my life began again. I awoke with a tiny lump on my neck that I couldn't ascribe to any insect. Had I eaten something carcinogenic? I used my phone to take a picture and compare it to all the other tiny lumps online. I saw hundreds of infected glands but couldn't find anything resembling my tiny lump.

I heard the upstairs neighbour releasing her morning piss. She remained seated for a moment before flushing, which I could also hear. Then, against my will, I remembered the shame of what had happened the previous day. The fountain and the fences made of human flesh, and my temporary disconnection from the now… My jeans were still experiencing aftershocks in the dryer. And I could no longer bear the thought of my sneakers, though they'd braved so much excrement. I wanted to walk in shoes that were pure! With all that human filth still clinging to me, a new pair of shoes might offer some relief.

I used the selfie mode on my phone to examine myself. I thought my neck was already too long compared to the rest of my body, and the tiny lump only marred it more. Its mysterious origins unsettled me. Indeed, the lump posed a threat. I considered various futures, the only common denominator being that none of them ended well for me. After all, skin is a safe and secure landscape, but it punctures quicker than you can imagine. I could conceal the lump with a polo neck, and no one would know the cruel fate that had chosen me. That is, until that fate was accomplished and I couldn't hide it anymore.

I could see my curtains whenever I stood on the pavement and looked up at my apartment. Two mint green strips of material, but the colour was only printed on one side. I'd hung them with the pretty side facing the street. I waved at them. Those curtains felt like family because I'd had them custom-made. No one else on the planet had these exact curtains. I'd bought the apartment with my share of the inheritance. It was a generous amount of money, but relatively speaking, because even after we'd received the settlement, my father was still dead. And his body was never found.

I was nineteen when I left home. This might sound obvious, but moving into a student share house was out of the question because I wasn't enrolled in university. And I'd have to wait at least ten years for access to public housing, so my only real option was to buy an apartment. It wasn't particularly easy. As a teenager, you have no concept of space (to say nothing of comfort), and I'm not sure I'd make the same choice now. The apartment is small, not quite forty square meters, and the living room is also the bedroom because I sleep on a mezzanine. Thankfully, as a pilot, my father had earned a fair amount of money, so my inheritance meant I didn't have to take out a mortgage.

In Old French, mortgage means 'dead pledge': an agreement you keep until you die.

Nesting urge. Vanity. Kamikaze.

I could smell the guinea pig cages inside the pet shop at the shopping centre. Some people like to give their children rabbits to familiarise them with mortality. Rabbits and hamsters, quiet and soft. Both animals only make noises if they think they're going to die, but a child wouldn't necessarily recognise an animal's fear. In contrast, guinea pigs are always making noises.

I bought a tube of ointment containing salicylic acid at the pharmacy. The writing on the package said the ointment healed blemishes. Only time would tell if my little lump fell into that category. I also stole two sweets, a strawberry and a Smurf, from the pick-and-mix jars. The remnants of them stuck to my teeth for a long time.

The spring collection at the shoe shop was disappointing. All the sneakers looked like spaceships. That's what is fashionable, said the shop assistant, though she didn't look like she believed that herself. Luckily, there were also different kinds of shoes, she reminded me. And upstairs, I would find the high heels and boots.

Urgent music was pumping through the speakers. Electronic Dance Music. I didn't want to surrender to the melody, but it was too late. I walked straight into the rhythm of the kind of music I hated. *Nononono*, said my internal voice, but it had no effect. I kept on walking to the rhythm and became a parody of humanity.

How long does the average tick bite last?

The high heels I liked the best didn't suit me. They gave me the kind of toe cleavage I couldn't reconcile with myself. I wandered through the aisle barefoot, passing loads of women I could potentially become; businesswomen in low heels and sporty women wearing laced-up hiking boots. Perhaps I could wear loafers, like a pensioner. My mother always said that shoes say a lot about a person. And now that I think of it, I could look as old as I wanted to.

Capuchin, anthrax, bastion.

I found them at the end of a rack of Wellington boots: bright purple and calf-length with a wondrous pair of heels that said tk, tk, tk. In other words, they were outspoken boots, the kind that confirmed the wearer's existence. The leather still had to mould itself to fit my skin, but that didn't bother me. A good pair of shoes will call out to you when you see it, and these boots had clearly chosen me.

How can I best describe the allure of these boots? Let me begin by saying they seemed otherworldly, as if made from an animal no normal person would ever wear. An environmental do-gooder wouldn't consider wearing shoes made from a cow, while someone more down-to-earth might draw the line at anything made from domestic pets. These boots had a snakeskin pattern embossed on the bright purple material. I'd never seen a purple snake and assumed some fictitious animal had inspired the scaly print. The boots symbolised everything deviant, exceptional, and improbable. The supernatural. The monstrous.

And they looked absolutely fantastic on me.

The shop assistant put my old sneakers in the box where my new boots belonged. She was mildly irritated. The security tag was still attached to the right-hand boot, but I refused to take it off. I let her squat beside my feet with the tool needed to release my boot from the tag, but it wasn't a quick process. While I was waiting, I surveyed the shop assistant's domain, which began at the counter and ended at a private door.

An enormous, framed photo was hanging on the wall behind the cash register. It was a portrait of the actress, Chloë Sevigny. I recognised her immediately. I'd seen a film in which she played a thirty-something woman who murdered her parents with an axe. But this photo had been taken while she was still young, and there was a certain vulnerability about her. She was posing with her mouth half-open, looking straight at the camera, but you could see some doubt in her eyes. Almost as if she was wary of how her face might look once the photo was taken. A lion's head applique had been stitched onto one of the shoulders of her jumper. I couldn't identify the jumper's designer. The fraying at the neckline betrayed the inferior stitchwork. Her haircut, on the other hand, was flawless.

Ginger, polyurethane, serenade.

When video rental shops still existed, my father was still alive, and I was always utterly obsessed with the videos displayed in the back room of the shop. Those rooms were always hidden behind red curtains that could only parted by movie fans over eighteen years old. The films in this section all explored the same subject: the human body's flexibility.

At thirteen, I was too young to venture behind the red curtain. But obedient people rarely have any fun. Whenever the staff were distracted by a client or a delivery person coming to re-stock the chips and tinned candy floss, I'd take my chance. One of the benefits of being small is that no one ever notices your comings and goings.

The men behind the curtain – and it was always men – would look at me whenever I entered their secret quarters. This was clearly because the teenage girls on the covers of the videos they liked to rent weren't actual teenagers. If the men were lucky, the girls they watched had only just turned eighteen. But more often than not, the cheerleaders and babysitters in question were all well into their late twenties. As for me, I was thirteen. I was the real deal, the thing men were searching for: innocence.

And yet, I could never truly compete with those actresses. Lusting after that kind of girl was condoned, but lusting after me was illegal. I wasn't even bordering on legal; surely none of the men behind the curtain would actually consider taking me home with them. But somehow, I knew that while they were back at home watching their sexy rentals, they would briefly think of me.

Which isn't to say that I was cool or mature for my age. It was quite the reverse; there's no way I could have been considered precocious. I looked at the covers of the videos behind the red curtain the same way I looked at lifestyle magazines with the other girls in my class. Women's magazines, which usually contained articles about fashion and work stress, also explored *pleasuring your partner* – a phrase we all found hilarious at thirteen. I didn't understand any of it, but I always laughed the loudest. When I was at the video shop, I got the same feeling I had when I attended sleepovers at my friends' houses; I was always worried I'd see or read something I didn't quite understand and be forced to react appropriately. Was I supposed to act like naked bodies impressed me? Should I smile at the sight of them or be repulsed? Or should I play the sensible card and feel nothing, or at least pretend I felt nothing? There hadn't been a moment in my life when I'd felt absolutely nothing.

I never tried to rent one of the forbidden films. With a face like mine, I'd never get the film past the checkout desk anyway. With my growing pains and virginal forehead, they'd see me coming from miles away! I'd once tried to rent a racy cabaret musical, and it turned into a real skin-of-the-teeth situation. The guy at the counter had phoned my mother to ask her permission, which she had given. But purely because I'd had to endure that humiliating scene, I immediately hated that musical. No, porn wasn't for me. Once I was done behind the red curtain, I'd have to re-enter the earthly world as subtly as possible. A world in which children's movies and comedies ruled supreme and sweets were sold by the pound.

I swear I once saw Chloë Sevigny on the front cover of a video behind the red curtain, but I couldn't be sure. There were so many blondes in the porn industry, and once you've seen enough of them, it's easy to get them confused. Innocent girls aren't quite as unique when there are so many of them. In any case, I still found the photo of Sevigny very beautiful.

There you go, said the shoe shop assistant. She looked me in the eye as she stood, which was as menacing as it was erotic. But that might also have had something to do with my daydream about the video shop.

Once outside, I threw the bag with my old sneakers into a bin. Tk, tk, tk said my new boots as they tapped against the paving stones. The sound of them made me so happy that I would have skipped all the way home, had I not felt too old for that kind of thing.

Parsley, goodnight kiss, misunderstanding.

The bridge opened for a passing boat…

The air was so grey… but my curtains were flapping in such a friendly way…

A tiny insect threw itself on the ground.

SLUGGISH. VULNERABLE. FAULTLESS.

They say grief is a finite process. Someone dies, something disappears (a union, a refuge), and the person left behind must make space for the emptiness. But how do you make space for emptiness? How much space does 'emptiness' require? It was a deadlock no one could solve. And the question itself is a bit of a cliché, but it's hard to avoid resorting to clichés when heartache is so ubiquitous. There's nothing rare about grief. It doesn't single you out or make you special. In fact, the opposite is true; your behaviour is utterly predictable. You invoke rituals that have been performed thousands of times before your grief even had a name. You re-evaluate the meaning of songs and flower bouquets. You comfort yourself with the jumpers and necklaces left behind, all the items that make you think of the person you lost, and you keep these things close to you, even when going through customs control at the airport, just to keep the past intact. As long as there's still a trace of the person you lost left in the living world, there's an open channel through which they could return.

Then, after a year or two, or whatever amount of time is considered appropriate for this kind of grief, you'll pack up that necklace and jumper and put them in storage with all your other precious things. Photos of your childhood and poetry notebooks filled with your juvenile handwriting. A place where you house all your talismans and the evidence of your past, the boundless space where the person you lost now belongs. And while you continue to fill the present with new urgencies (paperwork, deposit slips), there are only two days in the entire year when you can feel that person's presence again. On one of those days, you eat cake (or, in my case, marzipan petit fours); on the other, you burn a candle to remember them. But aside from this, you're pragmatic. You keep the dead at a distance.

At least, that is what any sensible person would do.

All those years, I kept my Black Box. I rarely used it, but I kept it in a pile of 'personal items' in my desk drawer, in the corner of the living room, by the window. My high school diploma and the folder I'd gotten from the notary when I'd bought my apartment were also kept in that drawer. Inside the folder was a document I had signed, rendering me the legal owner of the dwelling. I didn't have any other personal items. I wasn't the type to save 'things', except for the pelicans on my windowsill. They were exceptional, and they knew it. There was a haughty look in their eyes.

The day before yesterday was the twentieth anniversary of the day we buried my father. Or, rather, the day we buried the *idea* of my father. My actual father had disappeared. In that respect, he did feel truly dead: his disappearance from this earth was so undeniable that I couldn't even imagine seeing his ghost. Only once I became an adult did I start fantasising about the possibility of being reunited with him. Fuelled by films about lone-wolf types who leave their families, dye their hair and start new lives with nothing but some cash and a photo in their pockets, I dreamt of seeing signs of his second life. He might be running a convenience store in Brooklyn or Ghent. Or maybe he had taken on a completely different form and was now a news report or a flower.

Twenty years is a long time to have to live with someone's absence. Outside the context of grief, an empty casket doesn't mean anything. It's simply a show model for a potential future. An empty casket at a funeral is also proof that grief doesn't require an object. Even the suggestion of loss is enough to break a loving person in two.

Gag, bond, vicious.

I wish I could have had a normal adolescence.

But what does a normal adolescence actually mean? Is it staying up late and vandalising bus shelters? Keeping a diary? An adult can also do all of that. There was no need to get nostalgic if I could still do all these things as an adult. The only difference was that my body had changed. I could buy wine without having to show my passport, and I could smoke whatever I wanted.

At the same time, I remembered my old body hadn't completely disappeared. There was still a sliver of her left: the Black Box had kept her alive for me.

I've taken many photos since that night in front of the mirror. Starting with the usual suspects, the images that appear in every teenager's repertoire: close-ups of plants and bins on the street, then later moving onto portraits. The photographer whose course I took said that the most valuable images are often spontaneous. The trick is to capture people as they are, not how they want to be perceived.

An adolescent girl's power appears limited because her voice is still high-pitched, and her body is still small. But at the same time, without even knowing it, she determines the flow of consumer culture. The concerts she wants front-row tickets for, the films that make her swoon. She'll make so many adults rich with her desires. It's the language she uses and the dances she teaches herself. Her habits will come to characterise an era. Her style of clothing will have its own page on Wikipedia. And the most beautiful thing of all is that none of it is premeditated. Every choice she makes is the opposite of strategic; she is completely spontaneous and 'authentic'. Her impulses will keep entire markets afloat. Her poor decisions will be forgiven. Her community doesn't expect her to always get it right. As long as she's still a girl, every mistake is considered a brave attempt at something, and every bull's eye is a sign of precociousness. Her fear of failure is coquettish. Everyone knows that girls have always been the star of each era. Everyone, that is, except the girls themselves.

Every girl holds this power until she is called 'Madam' for the first time. And that day comes for every one of them, even for the most wilful girls. It can happen while standing at the train station or in a queue somewhere. Someone will suddenly address her with this honorific, sincerely and without a hint of sarcasm. And from that moment on, her clothing and hairstyle will be described as neutral, and the texture of her skin will broadcast a certain number of days, weeks, and years. 'Madam' – instead of 'Miss' – will become the title people will use to address her. And that's how it happens: the moment the girl is over. The curtains in her room will close, only to be opened in another room somewhere else, where a new girl has just asked her parents to gift her a pair of designer shoes for her eleventh birthday. From then on, that girl will characterise the next era. For the following thirteen years, the world will be hers.

Chloë Sevigny, I'd read on the internet, was once called the 'coolest girl in the world' by *Vogue*.

As a girl, I never saw a cent of the power I wielded. I was too consumed by grief and fear, both my own and that of others, and I was always expected to temper both emotions. Was it too late to demand my own fortune? I opened my desk drawer.

There were thirteen photos in total. Each time I clicked on a new one, the Black Box made my computer thrum. It had to dig deep to bring that girl back up to the surface. But my computer didn't give up and eventually dredged up every version of my younger self from her digital world. There she was, at seventeen years old.

My eyes were guarded in the photos. I was almost old enough to vote, but physically, I was still soft, a child without any sharp edges. Nature designed young people to be soft and smooth so that older people would want to protect them. The sweeter a child appears, the more precious their body. And a girl's body is extremely precious.

I'd held the camera in my right hand. And the left was on my hip, imitating a pop star on an album cover. The pose said *self-assured and sultry*, while my face said *guileless and fragile*. My inability to be seductive had inadvertently revealed my deepest secret: I was a girl aware of my allure, but I didn't know how to translate that into power.

I was sure some people would treat my teenage body like a rare possession, find it sweet and want to look at it… and would even pay a little money for the privilege.

I'd put the photograph of the little girl at the fountain on my desktop. I looked at her tiny hands, her red cheeks, and her nose, which had yet to take its adult form. She couldn't eat or use the toilet independently. She was still needy, in the sense that she needed people, but not the other way around, she wasn't yet able to influence the world around her. Her innocence had no double meaning. She was just sweet.

None of this applied to the photos of my naked, seventeen-year-old body. Her sweetness wasn't quite as apparent. She was also needy, but fulfilling her desires wouldn't be as straightforward, and in the years that led up to the taking of these photos, she'd come to understand that. I could tell from her pose that she'd already been corrupted. She'd learned what was expected of a woman's body if it wanted to be seen. The girl was mimicking the kitsch of predetermined desire. Adult women would laugh at her – *thank god I'm not like her anymore* – but they would also make sure that she got home safely with her clothes on and her knees intact. Some men would look at her but would only take her in their thoughts. Others would ask her what 'colour' wine she liked to drink.

I looked at the photos of my younger self and didn't know which group I belonged to: the people who wanted to protect her or the people who wanted to ruin her.

Rational isn't a word I'd use to describe myself.

THE PRESENT LOOKS BACK

The day that Google Street View launched, I went outside and waved at the sky. They had a camera in space that captured life on the streets. At least, that's what I understood it to be. I truly believed that this technology had the capacity to see me wherever I was in the world. All I had to do was step outside and go about my daily activities. On that first day of the future, I walked to the botanical garden, along the high street, and also visited the statue of the philosopher beside the water. I looked up and waved. Aside from the many attractions that filled my city, every potential web tourist who used Street View would see my enthusiastic greeting and think, *What a charming, happy girl.*

A man who was passing by waved back at me. I explained that I wasn't waving at him but rather, I was waving at an unknown eye in heaven, and even though there were more than enough sectarian jokes the man could make, he just laughed at me.

The photos have already been taken, sweetheart. No one's going to see you today.

Those were the days! – The years in which I was invisible and wandered through the days as if I were walking through a flea market. I was a miserable girl, and every day was like a new second-hand item that had already been chewed up and spat out by a more decisive person before I'd even gotten out of bed. I could look at things, touch them, and even bid on them, eventually paying far more than each item was worth. At cafés, I never dared to point at the croissant I actually wanted – yes, that one, the large one that's all light and fluffy in the middle, you can keep the small one up front – so all my moments of indulgence remained suboptimal.

But those days were behind me. I'd become the type of person who got out of bed early. In fact, I was out there forging plans while the rest of the world was still dreaming. I knew how to transform my old misery into money. And this time, I could name the price.

The misery in question was saved in thirteen files on my Black Box. How many films had I seen about timid girls who turned themselves into irresistible goddesses with only a few cosmetic interventions? As far as my seventeen-year-old self was concerned, her reception would depend on the context. Her pictures would be considered boring on a porn website, but she was definitely too naked for social media. In other words, the trick was finding some middle ground. I needed the dark web, the side of the internet where weapons were sold and passports were forged. Except I didn't want to sell any guns or forge any passports – it was my own teenaged body I was looking to sell.

Despite the many articles I'd read suggesting otherwise, the shady side of the internet wasn't so easy to find. First, you had to download an alternative web browser, because the 'normal' ones didn't allow you to access the dark web. And you also had to use a VPN, because your internet provider could raise the alarm if they found any suspicious activity on their network. Finally, you had to know which search engines to use, because the regular ones filtered out all the dubious websites from their results.

In other words, the dark web was inaccessible for a layperson like me. I had to compromise and find a place that bordered on indecent but was also easily accessed. My usual search engine knew where to look; I didn't even need a proxy.

Because right there, on the fifth page of search results, I found a website that caught my attention. It was part forum, part data bank. There was one section for sharing photos and videos and another section dedicated to discussion. The images ranged from pictures of shadowy cornfields (evidence of alien life!) to women wearing no clothes. I would publish my old self-portraits in the latter category.

It was already dusk outside. The neighbours had already switched on their heating, and my living room pipes were clanking. It sounded like a round of applause for my enterprising spirit. See, my apartment was confirming that I was on the right path. Don't back out now. Just create an account, yes, fill in your email and click on the box to confirm that you're human...

The website had only one condition: everything published on the site had to be created by the users themselves. Nothing could be doctored – or worse, plagiarised. But apart from that, they couldn't care less about the content itself. Under the guise of freedom of speech, everything was condoned. I clicked to check another box.

The pleasant feeling spreading through my belly told me that I was finally a part of something, that I was recognisable in some way, and I was exactly where I was supposed to be. But I shouldn't get too carried away; I'd only taken the first step. There was still a lot of work to be done.

To entice buyers, I offered the first photo for free. But I charged a small amount for the rest of the pictures. Nothing excessive. It was all well within the limits of what was reasonable. Users could pay me via a link posted underneath the first photo. Once I'd received the payment, they would automatically gain access to the file containing all the images. I read in the website's welcome email that if my photos were successful, I'd have to pay a percentage of my income to the web host. If no one was interested in the pictures, they'd be taken offline after three weeks to save bandwidth.

Everything sounded practical, easy, and self-explanatory.

The subforum where I published my photos was simply titled 'Girls'. It seemed to be the most popular subforum, with more than thirteen thousand unique uploads. I scrolled through them, and most of the photos were of women pretending to be younger, their hair in pigtails, wearing knee socks. It was a parody of youth. There were also lots of bikini photos of students who needed money for tuition. Their photos were accompanied by pleading messages and lists of their achievements. I *reeeeeally want to go to America to develop myself.*

The only images of underage girls were drawings. Manga girls with large eyes and equally large breasts, suggesting that when given a choice, most men would choose an adult woman after all. Small boobs like mine suggested a level of immaturity that was too creepy for modest desires.

A web counter in the top right-hand corner of the screen showed the number of users online at that moment: five hundred or thereabouts. And beside the title of every upload was a little

48

eye icon that showed how many clicks the post had gotten. My photos had barely been online for a minute, and twenty people had already looked at my younger self. The first reactions were also trickling in – a thumbs-up and a smiley face with hearts for eyes. I sold my first photos within the hour. Everything was going according to plan. It seemed like I could turn back time. My teenage self had been resurrected under the guise of entertainment and research.

Outside, it had grown dark. It was the hour at which children were already sleeping deeply, and adults were consumed by their fantasies – the perfect time of day for what I was doing.

I'd left my curtains open and could see myself reflected in the living room window. It was such a strange sensation: on-screen, I could see my seventeen-year-old self standing in front of the mirror, and at the same time, the window of my apartment reflected that same girl back at me. Only now, she was sixteen years older, wearing a polo-neck jumper and jeans, and underneath that, a set of underwear a seventeen-year-old girl would never wear: organic, white cotton. No leopard print or fruit motifs, nothing sexy, nothing sweet.

I don't have any visual memories of the years immediately following my father's death. But I can still smell the sweaty sports clothes that would sit in my locker unwashed for five weeks, but that I'd still wear to every PE class. I can also smell the buttery stench of frozen sausage rolls being re-heated for school lunches. And the scent of untreated wood in the school workshop, and the accompanying sawdust.

If the photos of my teenaged body were to advertise something in a fashion magazine, it would be a perfume based on these scents. I could put a little plastic strip on my naked hip,

49

which could be peeled open to sample the perfume. The reader would smell it, perhaps even use their index finger to spread it all over their wrist, and after they had thoroughly experienced the perfume, their instinct – which is, after all, guided by scent – would be to say: *No, this isn't for me.*

But the eye, that indulgent organ, would be curious about the possibilities my soft skin and searching gaze implied, and let itself be led by that.

One of the forum users wrote underneath my photo that I was horny. As powerful as I was, I still felt sorry for him. This person didn't know the difference between pleasure and fear, two forms of arousal that appear almost identical on the surface but are fundamentally different at their core. He thought I had taken those photos for the fun of it. I suspected that if I were to examine his romantic life, I'd uncover loads of issues. Or perhaps that was why he was looking at my photo on the internet instead of sitting in a pub, beside an adult woman who called him 'sweetheart'.

The pipes in my living room stopped rattling. Everything that needed to be said had been said. The night fell silently.

It was just me and the light from my screen. Every time I refreshed the forum page, the number of users that had visited my page increased. The first few hundred visitors made me anxious, as if I were just about to enter an exam hall. By the time the number of visitors had climbed into the thousands, it all felt too surreal to summon any emotions. Or maybe people get used to that kind of attention very quickly. Refreshing the page became a subconscious act. The forum faded into the background, and my teenaged body turned into a shadow, which became an animal, then a hand. In my reflection in the window, I saw an alternative future, an adult life that deviated from mine:

In this version of the present, I was a sensible person. I immediately put my bread in the freezer after buying it and never let it grow mouldy in the pantry. I packed my shopping strategically, with litre bottles at the bottom and porous fruit on top. And I had a lover who helped me carry it all. At night, we slept beside each other, my lover and me. The unholy sounds my apartment made didn't bother me – the branches that scraped against the window, the tapping of the old radiator (no applause now, just an indication of time swallowing daylight). All sounds irrelevant to a body that knows no fear. I didn't have to brace myself when plugging the vacuum into the wall. I didn't mind the sound it made. On Saturdays, I bought bags full of fresh vegetables from the local market. I knew exactly which vitamins I lacked, purely from my hair's elasticity and the structure of my skin. I owned a serum for every part of the day, and I was never dehydrated. My father was still alive. He would only pass away when he was old and grey, and the cause of death would be something very normal, something I could easily explain to acquaintances without being overwhelmed by the atrocity and randomness of the story I was sharing. My cupboards were filled with photo albums. Countless photos, neatly sorted into little plastic pouches, confirming all the phases of life I'd known. If I had any questions about an item of clothing I'd worn, or a distant relative, I could just call or even visit my parents for answers. In any case, I'd see my parents often. We'd wander through the dunes together on sunny days, then drink coffee at a beachside café. And it would be my treat because I had an excellent job with a generous salary, and I wanted to use my fortune to show how much I loved them.

When I woke up each morning, I would know precisely what to expect, and the first morning that this wasn't the case, someone would notice.

WITH EACH LOSS,
THE BODY BECOMES MORE PRESENT

I woke up with my cheek against the mouse pad. The pad's texture had left an imprint on my skin, which looked disturbing, but felt quite nice to touch. Despite my resolution to become a night owl, I'd managed to fall asleep – but had remained active in the digital world.

While I had been sleeping, my photographs had garnered more than five pages of responses. Five whole pages just for me! Or rather, for the body I'd once inhabited. All of this had happened overnight. It felt like I'd opened my curtains on a summer day to find the landscape covered in snow.

But with success comes resistance. Aside from the emojis with hearts for eyes and messages from people who appreciated my photos, there were also forum visitors who had their doubts about the young woman staring at them through the mirror. They wanted to know: how old was the girl? Which country was she from? Had she given her permission before the photos were published online? And how had I gotten my hands on the pictures in the first place?

One user with the screen name Little Weasel, whom I suspected was also a woman, had simply posted a frowning emoji. Only later did I notice the little envelope blinking at the top of my browser. Little Weasel had sent me a private message calling me a pervert.

Still, for all the disapproval, no one seemed to have reported my photos as inappropriate. It wasn't as if this was a case of manipulation or plagiarism. I giggled at how easy it had been to turn myself into a product.

But Little Weasel wasn't the only critical voice. One of the forum moderators, whose username was just a row of numbers, had also sent me a message, asking how I'd come across the images. Are you the girl in the photos? Because if I was, he pointed out that I should have checked the box verifying I was over eighteen years old on the registration page. If I wasn't the girl in the photos, had I taken a child's self-portraits and posted them on the forum as if they were my own, making a decent amount of money in the process? In both cases, I'd made a mistake: either I had failed to adhere to the forum's incredibly lenient terms of use, or I was a purveyor of a strange and melancholy genre of child pornography.

And the responses just kept streaming in. I was getting at least one email per hour from someone who had bought my photos and wanted to see more, buy more, own more. These requests made me uncomfortable, not because the people making them were so shameless in their desire for a teenage body, but because they desired a version of me that no longer existed – or perhaps never had.

Little Weasel's insult wasn't the only one I received. And evidently, it wasn't acceptable to ignore these messages, as I had done, so now my adversary wanted me to atone for it. It started when Little Weasel noticed that I was online but clearly hadn't found her insult worthy of a response. Her resentment (or was it something else?) made her bombard me from every direction. She posted underneath my photos, sent me direct messages, and even sent me texts. Apparently, the telephone number I'd used to register for the website had just been casually published on my profile for all to see. While registering, I seemed to have forgotten to check the box required to keep my personal information hidden, meaning that everything was now 'public'. This meant I was now being harassed by a stranger who had questions (*Who is that girl???*), and that stranger was also refusing to accept my silence. It was awful! Missed calls from unknown numbers kept coming in at a dizzying pace. By the end of the afternoon, it felt like the little green light on my phone was holding me hostage. And I hadn't responded to the moderator's message either.

What would my father think if he saw me like this? Would he still want me as his daughter? He'd once kicked Sister out of the house for the night because she'd worn a G-string. The string had peeped out above the waistband of her jeans while she was mounting her bike, and my father, who'd been keeping a close eye on her, had locked and bolted the front door in protest. Then there was the time I went shopping when I was eleven and had sneakily thrown a women's magazine into the shopping cart. Once we were home, the magazine was discovered and thoroughly scoured for any indecent content before it was returned to me in half its original state. My father had torn out all the sex tips and articles on relationships.

The hours stretched, night fell, and the little green light would not stop flashing. My photos had earned me almost one thousand euros in a day, but I couldn't enjoy it because I was so scared. Why couldn't all these people just sit and look at me in silence? If they continued attacking me like this, the situation could get out of hand.

I needed to regain control. After all, it was my teenaged body, and they were my photos. The fact that people had paid money to view them didn't mean that my body automatically belonged to them. They couldn't say a thing about me. My past was mine, and that was that!

Just as I was about to compose a nasty threat in response to Little Weasel, my revenge was interrupted by a mild... let's call it 'commotion', in the hallway.

It was early in the morning, so early that it was still dark outside, while it was already May. It couldn't possibly be the mail being delivered. In any case, the person who delivered the mail to my building never went beyond the ground lobby. The sounds seemed to be coming from my floor. No doubt about it, there was a stranger out in the hallway. Could it be one of my paying admirers, or worse, Little Weasel?

I went to the door and squeezed my feet into my new boots. I'd left my kitchen window open overnight, and a cold breeze nipped at my ankles before I could zip up my boots. A homeless person might have come inside seeking warmth. This kind of thing happens occasionally in centrally located buildings like mine. A stairwell offers very little in terms of comfort, but sometimes, the city forces us to make the uninhabitable habitable.

There didn't appear to be anyone in the hall when I looked. This gave me some comfort, because whatever was causing the noise clearly wasn't on my floor. But I was also concerned, because this obviously meant the noise originated from a place that was invisible to me. Invisible, that is, unless I decided to investigate. I listened desperately at the door of the apartment next to mine. Were the neighbours already awake? Could I hear the percolator or voices on the television? No – it was dead silent. If someone were to bash my brains out, there wouldn't even be any witnesses.

Fear gave me the sudden urge to laugh. I had to cover my mouth because if my neighbours were awake, then they certainly shouldn't hear me laughing to myself in the hallway. A person who has a laughing fit in the stairwell at the crack of dawn would be too weird. It would only make me seem more suspicious.

In a burst of strategic insight, I realised that taking a weapon with me was probably a good idea. Years ago, I'd seen a film where the protagonist had temporarily blinded the enemy with flash photography. Maybe I could do something similar. If bad intentions were at play, then the flash on my camera could allow me to escape. And if I was able to escape with the camera intact, then I could also end up with an excellent action photo.

I strode down the stairs with my camera in hand. The heels on my boots made soft *ka-duk, ka-duk* sounds on each step. It was neither night nor day, and I had barely slept because Little Weasel had decided to stalk me digitally. I was deathly afraid and dead tired, but ready for the unknown.

There was nobody in the stairwell. The foyer was also empty, though the plastic bags piled up on the footpath reminded me it was garbage day. Apart from this, there was nothing that made me confront my mortality. I'd have to make do with the nascent grooves in my forehead and the knowledge that there was probably a murderer lurking on the floor above mine.

When I reached the top floor, it was also silent. I listened at the door for a moment: maybe my upstairs neighbours had been out and just gotten home. Beside their front door was a cabinet filled with shoes. Just like most people who live on the top floor of a building, the upstairs neighbours had assumed that no one would ever come to their floor and filled the landing with their personal belongings. But my appearance on their floor completely undermined that assumption. The sensor light responded to my body and switched on, revealing that no one had been hiding in the shadows.

But once I was back at my own front door, I heard another small commotion. It didn't sound like thunder. It was more like a soft material encountering another, rougher material. I held my camera at the ready. This is the moment, I told myself. Here is the terrifying future your past has led you to. In the next few minutes, you must be uncompromising.

I took a photo. The flash bounced off the acrylic handrail, which was dreadfully shiny. Then I heard the rumbling noise again, but it sounded faster, more urgent this time. I looked up.

In the corner near the window was an enormous black moth. His wings – I assumed it was male, given that he'd just decided to let himself into the building – were noisy and nothing like a fairytale. This beast had nothing in common with the sweet butterflies found in children's books, which were always colourful and full of wisdom. Instinctively, I crossed myself. It was entirely possible that I was standing face to face with a reincarnated soul. It could even be my own father, with his jetlag and everything, coming to wake his daughter at an unreasonable hour.

Are you there? I asked the moth. Do you know how to speak human?

The insect answered by furiously and absurdly fluttering his wings through the stairwell, which I interpreted as a 'yes'.

My longing for paranormal contact intensified.

In a state of deep distress, the differences between the living and the dead can be bridged, even between two different species. Hearing birdsong at the right moment can foretell a good day, a funny dog video can offer the viewer immeasurable comfort, and even clattering vertical blinds have the potential to harbour messages from the dead.

My god, I thought, they've put my own father in a moth!

Do you recognise me? I asked the moth. I'm your daughter. You taught me how to do long division.

...

Your name was the third word I learned. My first word was 'juicy', then it was 'Mama' and only after that did I learn how to say your name. I hope that doesn't bother you. We had the same favourite dish: gnocchi with aubergine. I believe that made up for a lot of the bad blood between us.

...

I have your eyes. Sister inherited Mama's brown eyes, but mine are bright green. Now that I think of it, my eyes are the only thing of yours I still have.

...

I've also tried to find you in other parts of myself, but you weren't anywhere to be found. You never had breasts or a bum. And actually, neither do I. My breasts have always been incredibly small, and you can be sure I blame you for that.

...

And despite the rare pelicans decorating my windowsill, I'm not at all happy, and for that I also blame...

'Would you mind keeping it down please?'

The door to the stairwell flew open, and the woman who lived in the apartment above mine was standing on the threshold.

Sorry, I answered. I thought I saw my father.

The neighbour threw a glance at my camera. I considered taking a sneaky photo of her to scare her off, but I was overcome by common decency, even at such an indecent hour. But after wishing me a somewhat cynical 'good morning', my neighbour returned to her lair.

Once I was alone again, I could no longer find the moth. I scoured the entire stairwell, using the flash on my camera so frequently that I emptied the battery. And my boots returned to making their familiar *ka-duk, ka-duk* sound on the steps as my search took me to every floor in the building, but I never found my father.

I SHIT THROUGH THE BARS ON
MY WINDOWS AND FORCE MYSELF
TO BE MORE PRESENT.

When you find yourself processing a significant loss, it can help to give yourself a gift. I don't mean a treat, because those are only meant for birthdays. Instead, you should view it as borrowing something from another life, or from another person who isn't having as hard a time as you. Give yourself something that definitely wouldn't fit an older version of you, but still makes you feel good enough to catch a glimpse of another, less miserable version of yourself – a version that has ostensibly lost less.

My Sister got a tattoo, my mother got a dog, and what did I get? I gave myself a life as a city girl. I moved to the city centre, immersed myself in 'trends' and took up a hobby that was worth something on the internet (photography). I was too comfortable to make it my primary discipline. Though I had experienced an immense amount of grief, I'd never actually had to fight for anything. My bills were always covered, and I had enough money to live a carefree life. I used my inheritance to buy smoothies, face masks and Pilates lessons. I didn't need to convince anyone of my right to live amongst the other city women. Not anyone, that is, apart from myself.

That afternoon, I went out to get a coffee. The café was new and had a photograph of a croissant hanging in the window. The girl operating the espresso machine was also relatively new: her forehead was utterly devoid of wrinkles, and she'd never heard of a dirty chai. It's a chai latte with a shot of espresso, said the other girl, who was standing behind the cash register. I presumed she was the manager and wondered if she was also responsible for the croissant hanging in the window.

I waited to the right of the counter for my coffee and watched the younger girl navigating the espresso machine. A mix of spices was retrieved from a pot, milk was frothed. My order was served steaming hot in a cup without a lid, and to my surprise, the girl had drawn a heart in the foam. Her small act of kindness wasn't lost on me. I was also given a larger cup than I'd paid for.

Enjoy, said the girl who'd made her first dirty chai that afternoon. I nodded at her, and our interaction came to a natural end.

Outside on the street, I saw she'd also written my name on the cup. That heart, the size of the cup and my name – the way all these things confirmed my existence overwhelmed me. At the bus stop, I saw an ad for a sunny travel destination and threw the cup at it as hard as I could. Then I got on with my day.

I boarded the bus and took the seat next to the emergency hammer. You never know when you'll need an emergency hammer, but you'll want to be sat in the right spot when that moment arrives. Feeling safe is an integral part of internal progress. If you feel threatened, your thoughts can become the cage that traps you.

There were always enough people on the inner-city public transport system who were suffering from their internal progress, or rather, their lack of it. Every day was a rehearsal for the following day, when precisely the same thing was bound to happen all over again. There was room for some variation on the weekends and during school holidays, but it would only be a temporary deviation from the weekly schedule. As soon as they were back on that schedule their days marched on, relentless and mundane. And the people on the bus were supposed to be the tireless participants in the system. The true purpose of their lives, the big premiere of the thing they'd practised and prepared for in their dreams, would, after all, have to remain a dream.

There were some part-time workers, each absorbing one final song through their headphones before they had to relieve their colleagues and give themselves over to another afternoon of work obligations. And there were day-trippers, sharing facts about the city they were visiting for the day, suppressing a slight nervousness about all the unknown things they would encounter. And the hypochondriacs, with their bellies full of paracetamol, on their way to the doctor's office, hoping to be prescribed something stronger.

And then there was me. I was also sitting on an inner-city bus on that particular day, which I will now describe. I was going somewhere I didn't go every day, even if the destination was familiar and quite close.

I was on my way to see Sister, who worked at a solicitor's office in the southern part of the city. Thanks to the employee information listed on the website, I knew that she held open office hours on Wednesdays, which meant it was her duty to help whoever happened to drop in looking for legal advice, including her long-lost sister.

Earlier that day, I'd been banned from the online forum. The moderator had sent me a message saying that he didn't appreciate my lack of response to his previous message. He'd also let me know that he thought my photos were disgusting. His message was the first thing I saw when I finally woke around eleven. I still felt exhausted from my encounter with the moth in the stairwell. The green light on my phone was flashing urgently.

It was a nasty message, and at first, I didn't want to believe it, but I was denied access when I tried to log into the forum. A message appeared on my browser: *You have been banned from our forum due to inappropriate behaviour.* The message was accompanied by an annoying sound, a bell ringing in the ugliest minor key. It was all very sudden and creepy. I was quite shaken! In one fell swoop, my second girlhood, just like my first, had disappeared without a trace.

This will make me sound vain, but the whole situation reminded me of a photo I'd seen during my photography course. The teacher had given a talk about it under the guise of teaching us about 'impossible images' and 'saying the unsayable'. His righteousness had sounded forced during the lecture, so I'd switched my attention to another channel. The clatter of a passing tram, the compulsive movements of one of my classmates: jiggling his knee, constantly clicking his pen. Kevin Carter, a photojournalist, took the photo in question, and it won him the Pulitzer Prize for photography. It was a picture of a starving little boy who had fallen to his knees while just behind him, an enormous vulture was eyeing the boy as if he were a bowl of fresh gnocchi. It was a gruesome image: a portrait of an animal, unaware of human morality, looking at its prey.

But, the photography teacher suggested, this awful picture had achieved something. A small army of activists was awakened when the photo was printed in *The New York Times* in 1993. Suddenly, everyone wanted to donate money to humanitarian causes. Shipping containers filled with food were sent to South Sudan. The famine had to be stopped! At least, until a new disaster unfolded in another part of the world, and everyone forgot about the little boy and the vulture.

We wanted to know what Carter had done after taking the photo. Well, said the photography teacher, people asked Carter that same question when the image was published. Back then, he told people he'd shooed the vulture away but hadn't done anything beyond that to assist the child. He said he felt ashamed to admit it, but he had taken the picture and left without even stopping to ask the child his name. And, god, he had no idea what had happened to that boy after the vulture had disappeared.

Four months after he won the Pulitzer Prize, Carter had gassed himself in his car. In his suicide note, he'd written that he could no longer cope with all the evil in the world. Our teacher didn't want to clarify whether the vulture or Kevin Carter himself was the evil one. He clearly idolised Carter, and from the way he talked, I could tell that the rest of the story painted an uncomfortable truth. The anecdote about the photo had only been intended to stoke our enthusiasm for photography and to illustrate the potential impact our work could have in the future. We, too, could have our work published in major magazines. We, too, might also win prestigious awards.

The other students had practically licked their lips at the thought of all this, but I had frowned. It's entirely possible that my very first forehead wrinkle was born during that class. The only conclusion I could draw from Carter's story was that photography couldn't save lives, but you could destroy someone's life with a photo. And that anyone who knew this and still aspired to be a photographer was probably incredibly narcissistic.

Exhibit A: I'm around eleven years old, and I'm watching my father giving Sister a stern lecture using expressions he seems to have picked up from the television. *This isn't a charitable organisation! This is not a hotel!* He yells these things whenever Sister puts her feet on the table or opens a new packet of crisps while there's already an open packet in the pantry.

Exhibit B: It is December, the night before Christmas. My mother had gotten all the presents beautifully wrapped at the shops and hidden them on the car's back seat, so Sister and I wouldn't find them. I should tell you that we were the kind of people who always opened cupboards out of curiosity. That night, tempted by the logos on the wrapping paper, someone had broken into the car and taken all our presents. Even the gingerbread men, which were probably frozen solid and impossible to eat, hadn't been spared. My mother had panicked: *What was wrong with people these days?* Most of the popular toys she'd bought us – the dream dollhouse, the board game with buttons that lit up – would likely be sold out everywhere by Christmas Eve. That year, Sister and I were given chocolate, socks, a card game, and a lesson in managing our expectations.

A few seats in front of me on the bus, a father was explaining to his son that red was the colour of danger, both in the natural and in the human-made world, and that the child should never just randomly pick red berries. He said red usually meant its poisonous, so you shouldn't take any risks when it comes to red fruit.

Another stoplight. Thankfully, this one turned green almost immediately, and when we went around the roundabout, we passed a squashed pigeon. An opportunistic seagull – is there any other type of gull? – was helping itself to the pigeon's kidneys and her tiny, clogged city heart. *Traitor*, I whispered at the window.

Exhibit C: There was a stray cat in Romania. It was the first time I'd gone somewhere other than France for a holiday. Sister and I had followed her around our hotel's cul-de-sac, and she'd led us to a nest of kittens. We played fearlessly with those kittens, completely unaware of the parasites stray cats can carry. They were soft and noisy. Naturally, we loved them. We'd given them temporary names, which we uttered with panache whenever we knew our parents were listening. I *really* wanted my own little cat.

But the mother cat saw us as a threat. She hissed at us, and when that didn't appear to have any effect, she began making this deep, growling noise that sounded a bit phlegmy. It didn't impress us very much. The radiator at home produced sounds that were far more intimidating. It would have taken a machine gun to dampen our bravado. Visiting the kittens became our ritual for the rest of our stay in Romania. It was our daily dessert after a main meal consisting of a swim in the pool and a visit to a historical site or local market. After four days, the mother cat had had enough. She decided to evacuate the entire nest to stop her kittens from smelling like children's hands. With the skin of her babies' necks between her teeth, mother cat searched for a new, much safer shelter. Eventually, she chose a place on the other side of the wall that bordered the cul-de-sac. We couldn't see what was on the other side of that wall, but we knew that she would rather stay there than endure any more of our hysterical, girlish love.

Right before the end of our vacation, we came across the kittens' bodies, which were as rigid and stiff as door stoppers. There was a parking lot on the other side of the cul-de-sac, where rats scurried around.

This is what happens when you want something a little too much and pursue it beyond reason, our mother said to us as we cried on the backseat of the car and couldn't be cheered up with a single crossword puzzle. We'd gotten it so wrong and unwittingly sabotaged our dreams, all because of our Disney-like view on the situation. We never did get our own kitten.

The boy on the bus still had a Disney-like view of the world. His father looked at him endearingly, which is the only way a young parent ever looks at their child in public. Children are only ever comical, clever, or feisty between the ages of two and ten. That little boy, with his oatmeal complexion, had obviously never tasted a ginger shot or smoked a cigar. He was virginal in every sense of the word. He had a father to warn him about the dangers of eating red fruit.

Ultimately, the incident with the mother cat didn't traumatise us at all. None of the things that Sister and I experienced during our childhood – the car getting broken into, the dead kittens – had enough of an impact to damage us for life. Even Beanbag, the bereavement therapist, would say we had a *good childhood*, despite everything. There were ice creams and animals and holidays.

At the next stop, a girl of around sixteen boarded the bus. She was listening to music on her smartphone without any earphones. The song featured an upbeat male voice singing *I know* you want it, which was an amusing sentiment for the situation (a city bus on a Wednesday afternoon) and the girl (who had an aura of general disinterest).

Oatmeal Boy's father frowned. I thought he was going to say something about the girl and her loud music, but he seemed too timid to open his trap. He wanted to protect his son from 'questionable influences' but clearly wasn't about to throw himself in the line of fire. Work it out yourself, you wimp, I thought to myself, and shifted my attention elsewhere.

Just two more stops before we reached our destination. At the penultimate roundabout, I began to feel a little light in the head, as if I was dizzy and also in love. I had forgotten whether my Sister had freckles or if she voted far-right or if she was a vegetarian. Maybe she'd get angry or try to humiliate me when she saw me.

The girl without the headphones got off the bus, and the father looked visibly relieved. I wanted to kick him in the head because his worries weren't half as big as mine.

Can I eat green berries, Papa?

Sometimes. But when a fruit or berry is green, that usually means that it isn't ripe.

The bus spat us out onto a platform where trams, metros and other forms of transport converged. Children, workers and patients were all following their chosen routes or taking a break at the snack bar nearby, where lukewarm croquettes were served in little cardboard caskets. They dreamt of ragout and unsuspecting palates.

The platform wasn't far from the building where my Sister worked. It was quite a large office, located in a section of the

69

city that was essential to the country's economy. Naturally, it had its own well-appointed bus stop. Most people who commuted to this particular bus stop wore business shirts and fabulous designer shoes.

It was lunchtime, the snack bar's serving windows were open, and everything smelt like mayonnaise and breadcrumbs. It had been a tactical choice to visit at this time of day. Even my Sister had to eat lunch. As far as I knew, she couldn't ignore her body's basic needs.

The automatic revolving door set the desired walking pace: carefree, but not entirely relaxed. My natural pace didn't quite fit the rhythm, and I strode through the building to an unusual beat. A sign hanging next to the door thanked me for not smoking.

The reception room was busy. There were groups of hungry lawyers everywhere, and they appeared to be choosing their lunch companions based on nothing more than shared ambitions and similar feelings of guilt. They moved through space like shoes in a washing machine. Ka-duk, ka-duk. I approached the front desk.

No, I didn't have an appointment, but I did know my Sister's first name and room number (which I'd googled beforehand), so I was allowed to walk through the turnstile. Then, a receptionist accompanied me to the lifts, used her pass to activate one of them, and sent me up to the correct floor. Activate was the word the receptionist used. She seemed to find herself incredibly important.

The carpet on the eighth floor was vermillion-coloured, a bold choice for a firm that deals with dead family members. inheritance law was printed on a metal sign next to the lifts.

My Sister's secretary was wearing a necklace with a rose quartz pendant. The rest of her outfit wasn't worth mentioning. Was rose quartz considered fashionable office wear, or was she attempting to give others a subtle glimpse of her true nature? I suspected my Sister's secretary was too kooky for the legal sector and too much of a drama queen for a more prestigious career.

Can I help you? she asked.

I'm here to see my Sister. We're going to have lunch together – my treat.

Ah, yes. And which name would the appointment be under?

I don't have an appointment. I'm her sister. She has open office hours today.

One moment, said the secretary. She gestured to a row of chairs beside the window. I didn't sit down but allowed myself a sip of water from the water cooler, which said 'blub' after I'd filled my cup. The cup happened to have the same shape as a party hat.

While looking out the window, I was hoping to catch myself feeling a little dizzy again, but I didn't feel anything, and also worried that I might be a bit depressed. I thought about the images and ideas that had recently occupied my mind. Then I knew I was depressed, and the certainty of that calmed me and was even satisfying enough to make me smile. The party hat was a small cup of nothing; I emptied it in two sips. Everything was small that day.

The secretary returned from her unknown mission. She motioned at me to come closer.

The solicitor is unable to see you, she said to me.

Why?

She has another appointment.

It's lunch time.

Yes, she's attending a business lunch.

When will she be back?

The solicitor is unable to see you, she repeated.

A solicitor, that's what my Sister had become. A kind of bureaucratic grave digger. A person who earns their money when someone else's light is extinguished.

Vulture. Herring gull.

I thanked the secretary for her time. I said it with sarcasm, which I instantly regretted because, after my rude finale, I had to go back and ask her to give me access to the lift. The secretary stayed furiously silent as she held her pass to the sensor.

Outside, the last few lunchtime pangs of hunger were being satiated. Around the corner from the office was a food truck selling falafel. A couple of men in white shirts stood around, ravenously waiting for the deep fryer to signal that their food was ready. One of them, the guy standing at the front of the line, pressed too hard on the pump that delivered garlic sauce to the food truck's customers. A dollop of sauce landed on top of his beautiful shoe. As far as I could tell, he was surrounded by people who would be willing to get down on their knees and lick the sauce right off it.

I promised myself the next time I saw my Sister, I'd meet her at a more neutral location, like a botanical garden, a schoolyard or a funeral home.

THE PAST IS BECKONING ME
THROUGH MY LETTERBOX

The bus ride home wasn't as interesting as my ride there. I wanted it to rain, but it wouldn't rain. We passed a man throwing up beside a garbage bin, and I was reminded of the evening of my thirty-third birthday, which I'd celebrated at the annual fun fair. It was a chic version of a fun fair, where people drank mojitos instead of beer. It had become a tradition to take the lime wedge served with your drink, squeeze out the juice, and then throw it over your right shoulder. This was supposed to bring you good luck for the evening's gambles, but the high alcohol content of the drinks probably also contributed to the locals' daring. By that, I mean the people in attendance generally spent more money and were quicker to disappear into the bushes with each other, which was always good for the general vibe.

I went to the fun fair alone because I went alone every year. That was also tradition, because the point of the fun fair was to meet new people. And that's exactly what had happened throughout my entire adulthood. I would start the evening alone and end it in a construction-site office or hotel room with one or more of my fellow singles.

Except the year I turned thirty-three, it was different. No one wanted to have anything to do with me. When I approached people to chat, they acted like I didn't exist. I was wearing a dress which made my bum look good, despite its flatness, so my appearance couldn't have been the issue. Maybe – and this was the most likely scenario – they thought I was too old to be staggering around the fun fair alone.

Half an hour before midnight, I'd somewhat tipsily stumbled into the fortune teller's tent. It was the only tent at the fair I'd always been too nervous to visit, because instead of all the usual bright lights, steel and chaos, it contained just one person.

The tent's interior was less spectacular than I'd imagined. I had expected various shades of purple and red, a crystal or two and enormous clouds of incense. Instead, there was just a collapsible table with an ashtray and a sudoku book sitting on top of it, which said more about the fortune teller's pastimes than about any prophesy. For fifteen euros, I could talk to her.

Show me your hands, she commanded when I sat down. And, because I'm so obedient, I did what she said. The fortune teller took a moment to look at me before she got to work.

I can already see it, she said after inspecting my hands for a few minutes. You have no brothers or sisters, and your parents are dead.

That's not right, I interrupted. I have a Sister. And only my father is dead. My mother lives with a dog who is constantly menstruating, but she doesn't want any contact with me.

Ah, so that's it.

You see, my mother only likes children and animals, so I was thrown overboard once I turned eighteen.

But back to your father's death… It came with an inheritance, right? Sooner or later, you're going to get a financial windfall. It's marked very clearly in your money line.

She used her finger to trace a vertical line on my hand.

Yes, that's right, I answered. I bought my house with the money I inherited from him – my apartment, I mean.

The fortune teller squinted slightly. I recognised this look: the meagre mist of jealousy. Plenty of people fantasise about receiving an inheritance the size of a mortgage from a distant uncle or aunt who leaves behind a fortune and can make all debt disappear with one posthumous snap of their fingers. Of course, it's rarely an immediate family member that dies in that kind of fantasy.

You'll need to be careful with the money, the fortune teller continued, because you will never have a steady job. That's also quite evident. This time, she pointed at the line closest to the centre of my hand.

Well, that's just great. No family and no job either. What more is there to life? Oh yes, there's love! What can you tell me about that?

About love?

Yes, what do the lines on my hand say?

Oh, sweetheart, you don't want to hear about that. It's not a particularly nice story. But let me finish by saying something positive. I see an animal in your future, an extraordinary animal. Are you thinking of getting a pet? A cuddly little bunny for company, perhaps?

Absolutely not. I can't stand animals. I won't tolerate any fur in my space. I find it tacky and tasteless. And I'd never bring home anything that makes sounds when I want silence. I really value my peace and quiet.

Oh, now that's a shame, because it means I haven't been able to tell you one good thing about your future. At least you don't have to worry about your mortgage. I hope you have a good night...

She laughed rather viciously, which I interpreted as a request to leave as quickly as possible. And with this, my spiritual consultation came to an end. While leaving, I heard the spark of her lighter. And I imagined her smoking a joint to mollify her rage.

Despite her lack of hospitality, I tried to think positively about the fortune teller's revelations. At least there was no typhus or human trafficking to be found on my hand. I should be grateful for everything I had. By the time I finally understood this, it was my birthday. I celebrated by riding on the swing carousel, which rotated so quickly that I was surprised I survived it. At home, I found myself genuinely smiling while brushing my teeth. A daddy longlegs crawled across my bathroom mirror, and I was in such a good mood that I didn't beat it to death.

Maybe, I thought, I would meet my true love very soon. That would be nice!

The bus lumbered over a speed bump. Just like the morning I'd met the moth in the stairwell, I suddenly started laughing very loudly. I was laughing so hard I literally had tears falling from my eyes. The bus driver looked at me in the rearview mirror. He wasn't my true love.

I exited the bus at the next stop and watched it drive away. The back of the bus appeared clumsy and cow-like. Farewell!

Once again, I found myself alone with my thoughts. At the kerb, I discovered that I was able to keep going, even in the face of all the familial rejection.

I walked past the local grammar school. The students in the schoolyard weren't smoking. The sun was at her highest point, and my boots said tk, tk, tk to the asphalt, but the asphalt didn't answer. From the edge of the schoolyard, I had a good view of all the different groups and personalities, and all the trends that went along with them. The kids weren't doing anything special, just staring at their shoes and phones. The older students wore shiny combat boots to mask their insecurities. The younger kids were too young to worry about that kind of thing and were wearing sneakers.

The students in the final year were standing in the corner of the yard. At least, I assumed they were in their final year because they looked like actual people. They wore jeans and black polo necks and looked a little like me. I lay a hand on the fake crocodile at my side, my camera bag. I might be able to pass off a picture of these kids as a clothed portrait of myself. If I posted a photo of a clothed kid online, I could be let back into the forum. The right image could cleanse me.

I stood at the edge of the schoolyard for a while, staring at the ejaculating penis that someone had drawn on the side of the bicycle shed. Nothing exciting was happening inside the shed. The penis had been drawn with a red pen and would be washed away by the rain within a year.

Hey! Who are you?

A woman around my age was walking towards me. She wore a scarf despite the sun and had probably been outside for some time. Perhaps she was a smoker. I tried to imagine her insides, her semi-charred lungs, and half the contents of her ovaries already gone. It was only once she was standing in front of me that I noticed she was wearing an expensive watch. This obviously left her vulnerable to people with bad intentions. Was she aware of that? I would never be arrogant enough to wear time on my body. It's like tempting fate or asking for trouble.

Her gaze was surly and impolite. She did nothing to prevent herself from being targeted. So, in protest, I refused to answer her question. The woman looked down at my purple boots, which now fit me perfectly. I acted as though I was ignoring her, but I was secretly studying her jawline to see if she was an addict.

Can I help you? she tried again.

It's important to know that an addict's jawline is as triangular as the jaw of a bat. In the bat's case, it's simply their anatomy, but with an addict, it's due to bone decalcification. And no, that's not the only similarity. Addicts and bats are both nocturnal animals. They take to the streets only once the rest of the city's animal kingdom is asleep, using that time to satisfy their hunger. One does it with their teeth and the other with a pipe or needle. It's impossible to keep the apples in your cheeks if you live that kind of lifestyle. You could even lose all your teeth if you don't watch out.

I looked at the woman to see if she still possessed all her teeth. Her mouth was closed, but she was wearing a name badge that said: Saffron Smit, Dean.

It was a strange name for an adult woman, let alone an authority figure. It was better suited to a teenager. Or a dog.

I'm going to have to ask you to leave, said Saffron.

I couldn't stop myself from laughing again. Suddenly, it was all too much for me: the ejaculating penis, the whole situation. What is this woman thinking? I thought to myself, What is she thinking?

If you don't leave, I'll have to call security.

It didn't need to come to that. I was already complying with her request. The children watched me as I walked away. At least, that's what I imagined, but I didn't turn around, so I couldn't know for sure.

At home, I was moving more quickly than usual through the stairwell. I was feeling sporty, like a warrior. As if I was going to live a very long life and only die once I was old. I nearly slipped in the hallway. The linoleum gleamed; the floor was cleaner than usual. Someone must have mopped while I was out. If I removed my boots, I could glide across the floor on my bare socks. What I mean is, I could glide… on my bare feet… in my socks.

The floor wasn't the only thing that looked different. A piece of tape was stuck to my front door. It was a dark blue label with the words FORENSIC INVESTIGATION printed on it. I was so surprised that I didn't believe it was real. But when I touched the tape, it felt like real plastic, and then I got scared.

My living room looked exactly as it had when I'd left. And my mezzanine also looked untouched, just like my bathroom, kitchen, blinds, and the pelicans.

It was only once I walked from the kitchen into the living room that I saw it. There was something different about my desk. My computer – along with all my photos, speakers, USB sticks, and second monitor – was gone. They hadn't left a single cable behind. And not only that: my Black Box was also missing.

The internet had betrayed me.

The last time I saw my Sister, she had just become a mother. I was twenty-five, she was thirty-one. I'd received a card with the birth announcement, even though I had only seen her sporadically since our family therapy session with the bean bag therapist. We weren't very close, but we were still family.

The girl – it was a little girl – was called Laurel. Just like me, she was named after a plant. Another ugly plant; she was no Iris or Rose. Laurel must be eight by now.

Mama and I rest between 12 and 3 p.m. If you'd like to come and count my fingers and toes, be sure to call first to let us know!

I went to visit them on a Wednesday. In hindsight, it hadn't been the best choice, because they already had other visitors. The father's sisters both had Wednesday afternoons off work, because their children didn't have school on Wednesday afternoons. And that particular afternoon, the whole bunch were sitting on Sister's sofa: two women, three children, a cacophony.

Coffee? Ginger tea?

The maternity nurse had plaited hair. She was just a girl herself. I could tell by her hips that she'd never given birth. I accepted the ginger tea but refused the biscuit. I had, after all, just become vegan.

Sister was wearing a dressing gown and had her hair in a knot. Her cheeks were pink, just like the tiny child in her arms. The girl was really very small. Her fists were only slightly larger than pebbles. I couldn't believe I was an aunt.

My little niece was all mouth. She did nothing but scream. It made the visitors nervous. Is she sad? asked the oldest child on the sofa, a boy of roughly seven. Maybe she doesn't want to be alive. Maybe she wants to go back into the belly. We should put her back in the belly.

The baby kept wailing. Sister tried to calm the little one. First, she used her finger, which was supposed to function like a dummy, but when that had no effect, she used her nipple. Sister shoved her dressing gown aside to reveal her breast without any shame. The nipple was large and dark. It made the other mothers uncomfortable.

The children all watched with interest as the nipple disappeared into the baby's mouth. After that, the baby was silent. There were a few little whimpers, but that was it. My niece was content.

See, there you go, said my Sister. She was also content, though in a more complex and mysterious way than the baby. She had brought a new body into the world; now, caring for it was her top priority. Her own nudity and the prudishness of her visitors didn't bother her one bit. I thought she was the most beautiful woman I'd ever seen.

By then, I was already carrying around the fake crocodile. I had scored the bag at a sale the previous autumn, but I'd owned the camera inside the bag for much longer.

I didn't think about it for long. My intentions weren't bad. I just wanted to capture that moment forever.

At first, I kept my distance. I wanted to photograph the moment exactly as I experienced it, from the same corner where I was sitting. But through the lens, it appeared less intimate than in reality. There was no way to translate it. I had to come closer to capture the intimacy I felt on film.

I squatted beside the chair where Sister was feeding her baby and leaned forward.

Hey! What are you doing?

Camouflage. Straitjacket. Horizon.

Everything happened very slowly in my memory, but in reality, it must have been mere seconds. I held the lens of my camera above little Laurel, so everything was perfectly in view. Her face, her mouth, and my Sister's nipple. It must have felt like such a threat to my Sister. I know for a fact that it did, because she reflexively kicked me with her right foot, which made me lose my balance and fall on my arse.

The fall didn't hurt me. But my Sister's disgust and her family-in-law's judgement still make me dizzy whenever I think about it.

I left without taking one sip of my ginger tea. I didn't get to hold my niece or see her again, because I wasn't invited to any more family gatherings or birthday parties after that. According to my Sister, I was *too anti-social and unpredictable*. She didn't want me around her child.

But if you were to look at all the photos I took of her that day, you'd probably believe we were very close.

There are days (and nights) when I am someone else. Someone with guts, who wouldn't hesitate to buy chocolate during a heatwave and bath bombs when it was raining. If I could only find the right channel, I could align myself with someone, a person from another time (or world) who doesn't have any bad habits or concerns about the ins and outs of everything. Without that empty coffin, I'd have become a different person. Can you see my silhouette burning behind the roller blind? I'm the kind of woman who has a solved Rubik's cube sitting on her windowsill, a woman who showcases all her successes and isn't afraid of failure, a woman who displays all the cards she receives for her birthday and Christmas on a clothesline (there are so many that the line spans the entire length of the room). I'm a woman who is capable of riding her bike straight over snails during their morning commute without the guilt keeping her awake at night. And because she has no doubts about the righteousness of her soul, this woman's position in the food chain is secure. We're all going to die – except for her, the flawless queen at the neighbourhood barbeque, an unequalled participant in the morning traffic, natural eyelash curler and wearer of watches. Her heart doesn't skip a beat when she sees chemtrails across the sky. She wakes up every morning and feels no fear, absolutely no fear.

A BALCONY SCENE

The woman put her shopping bags on the kitchen counter. On one side of the tap, there was a liquid soap dispenser filled with lavender hand soap. On the other side was a small compost bin. Most of her groceries had to go in the fridge, which stood in the corner of the kitchen, next to the washing machine. Sometimes, the woman dreamt of a larger house with an equally large kitchen and an island right in the middle, just like the families in American films. In that house, the dishwasher would be large enough to hold a frying pan, and she would have a separate cabinet just for herbs and spices.

In reality, the woman had to store her herbs in the pantry between the coffee filters and the rice. A family was something she didn't really have. She had a husband, and according to the city council, this counted as family, and they were taxed handsomely for it. But sometimes, at dinner, the woman found it a shame that there weren't more bodies sitting around the table.

The fridge was two metres tall. The woman had to stand on a little stepladder to reach the top shelf, where she stored all the water bottles. It was good exercise, lifting bottles filled with one and a half litres of water and holding them for a moment. If you did it a few times, you could even feel the muscles in your arms contract. She'd definitely feel it tomorrow, thought the woman, and it pleased her. She didn't need the gym at all.

The broccoli and the peppers went into the vegetable drawer. The cucumbers were slightly too long. The only place they'd fit was on top of the water bottles. And so up went the arms again, reaching far above her head.

The woman could hear her downstairs neighbours moving around beneath her feet. Or rather, she had only one neighbour living under her, just one woman.

Bottles of laundry detergent went into the kitchen cupboard, and the bag of croissants remained on the counter. The following morning, the woman and her husband would eat all the croissants in one sitting. All four croissants would go into the oven at the same time. The woman had read in the newspaper's cooking section that there was so much butter in croissants that you didn't need to put anything else on them, but she didn't heed that advice. The croissants would be spread lavishly with chocolate paste and jam.

She could hear furniture being moved around downstairs.

What was her downstairs neighbour's morning ritual? she wondered. What was her table like? There was just one body that bent and ate at it. Did the woman who lived downstairs even bother to cook for herself? Maybe she lived off microwave meals served in the same plastic containers they used in hospitals. There are only two options for thirty-somethings these days. They either live off microwave meals or they'll cook elaborate meals with all kinds of eccentric ingredients. The woman had also read this in the newspaper.

The bread went into the freezer. It wasn't needed just yet.

The woman had seen her downstairs neighbour in the stairwell a few days ago. She'd been stamping around, moving from floor to floor and talking to strangers before the day had even properly begun. Strangers who didn't even live in the building, strangers who weren't welcome inside. Dealers, the woman suspected.

Yes, the woman who lived downstairs invited dealers to come inside and allowed them to wait for her in the stairwell... Cocaine vendors with clandestine wares that offered the downstairs neighbour some temporary relief from her suffering. She probably had money problems...When the woman had encountered her in the stairwell, she seemed to be trying to convince one of the dealers that she was his daughter. The woman had to admit that it was a tragic scene. Witnessing that kind of despair in a fellow human is so sobering.

The woman picked up a bag of potatoes, the last item that needed to be put away. They belonged in the pantry. The potatoes had been too heavy to be put in one of the shopping bags, so the woman had carried them home alongside the rest of the shopping. *High-intensity interval training*, a voice inside her head had said.

Pitiful as it was, the downstairs neighbour's situation was also alarming. The woman and her husband hadn't taken out a mortgage to live among drug addicts. They wanted a quiet life in a building with reasonable service charges and a street party with all the neighbours a maximum of once per calendar year. Apart from that, the woman didn't want to have anything to do with her neighbours, but if there were any concerns about another tenant's lifestyle choices, then someone had to *raise the alarm*.

But who would be the person to sound the alarm? Who was responsible for an adult woman who should bloody well know what was expected of her?

Not me, thought the woman, before she undressed and stepped into the shower. Her shampoo smelt like jasmine; her body scrub promised her the skin of a newborn baby.

The boiler clicked. Warm water flowed. The woman rubbed the little hollow in her ankle, a spot she often forgot, and felt little clumps of dirt coming loose.

TOGETHER, I FALL APART

How would I look at myself if I were someone else? Would I be afraid if I came across myself on the street at night? No, I'd probably continue walking calmly along the same side of the street. From the outside, you couldn't tell I was damaged goods, that I always laughed it away whenever anyone mentioned the festive season and would hyperventilate at airports. In other words, a stranger would find my presence wholly unremarkable.

My fantasy did the rest. I left my body and gave it to another woman, someone who had never known grief. In my head, I gave her a name, a home and a lover. It all felt so real in the dark that I could even smell her body wash.

Because that night, I slept very little. Something was crackling inside of me. Call it desperation or just my conscience, but it felt like I'd never be able to relax. I climbed out of bed once an hour to check if the blue tape on my door was still real. Every time I felt the plastic cracking under my fingers, my anxiety would rise again, and I could hear my heart beating in my ears. The fourth time I checked it, I noticed my hands were shaking.

My father. Just the thought of him calmed me. His blood was in my blood, his eyes were in my eyes. He was in the way I could roll up my tongue. He'd pre-programmed every single disease I'd ever suffer from. I could eat as much broccoli as I wanted, run every day and add ginger to everything I drank, but if his genes wanted to destroy me, then sooner or later, it would happen. He was a part of me. If there was a sinister piece of tape stuck to my door and someone was trying to screw me over, then that must be what my father wanted to happen.

What would he have done in a situation like this?

The Black Box had been taken from me. If I'd still had the photos of my old body, then I could have compared them to the reflection of my new one. It would allow me to examine the process of transformation, the metamorphosis that had led me to this present and all the problems that came with it. Others would only notice the cumulative effect of the changes when the visual leap was obvious, like comparing a childhood photograph to your current state, but I could see the difference between last year's summer and now; I knew exactly how many moles I'd acquired. Give me a photo from fifteen years ago and one taken today, and I'll point out every discrepancy.

As a child, I used to hack live worms in half with my spade. I picked flowers from the gardens of strangers and pissed against bus shelters. On New Year's Eve, I'd throw fireworks into garbage bins and scream when they exploded. When my friends came to stay the night at my house, I'd lie about my parents' professions, and when I stayed at their houses, I'd steal all the magnets on their fridges and start eating my meals before their mothers even had a chance to sit down at the table. I also lied about the magnets, and would masturbate using cans of deodorant, hairbrushes, candles and the remote control for the television (just once). And I didn't wash these objects after I used them. I let others feel deep inside me, even when it was unwanted.

According to my school reports, I was a dominant child. How old was I when I became a responsible person?

Or rather, at what age did I *have* to be responsible?

My Sister had left home and was swimming in canals, and my mother was letting her dog bleed all over the kitchen tiles. In the meantime, I was the one who picked up the cleaning cloths. I opened the door whenever a neighbour came to complain about the amount of dog poo in the front yard. And I took the garbage bins out to the street for collection.

Now that I thought about it, I knew damn well how old I was when I became responsible.

After checking the tape for the sixth time, I decided not to climb back into bed. There was no point. I was never going to get any sleep. Reluctantly, I switched on the television. I saw footballers, trains, gold sellers and a repeat of the news report from earlier. The trivial situations calmed me but didn't distract me. On one of the international channels, I saw a former supermodel in a powerful position. She was the one to decide who would be the next supermodel. Ten girls with long legs and regular beauty routines stood at her service. Four of the girls had already been eliminated, and two of the remaining contestants had delivered a disappointing performance. They were about to be executed in a blue room. The trap beats that usually accompanied the onscreen action paused. The former supermodel began to speak: *Two beautiful girls stand before me, but I have only one photo in my hands...*

I switched off the television.

When looking at a large painting, the eye is always initially drawn to the foreground, but you always end up looking longer at what is happening in the background, examining the kind of complex details that are only discovered by the most punctilious of eyes. There's often a secret meaning hidden in the minor details, some of which are almost invisible. You can guess what it means, or you can try to explain it based on what you know – but that kind of knowledge is something most decent people lack.

On the internet, I'd seen men – and it was almost always men – who would count the days until their favourite underage stars turned eighteen. They would buy domain names and create web pages with digital calendars. When the girls – and it was almost always a girl – finally turned eighteen, the men would no longer have to feel guilty wanking over their photos – photos of the girls, I mean, who were at last women in the eyes of the law. Can you imagine the kind of implicit permission that age can give? The ease with which a body is transformed into a projection screen?

In what way was I more dangerous than these men? Why did my computer have to be confiscated?

Or was it nothing to do with the photos? Maybe this was about something else, something truly terrible that I didn't even know I had done. Perhaps I was innocent after all.

There was a moth in the bathroom which was only ever visible when I turned on the light. And in the mirror, I could see an anxious woman. It was unbelievable, the fact that I had become a woman. Twenty years ago, I hadn't even gotten my first period. I thought about all the men on the internet, the men who only desire women under the age of twenty-five. The men who claim not to be able to 'get it up' for women any older than that. The men who set their age limits on dating apps so low that they could potentially come across the profile of a nineteen-year-old girl, even though they are over forty themselves. I could wash my hair with a restructuring shampoo. And while washing my body, I could pay special attention to my armpits and my anus (the bathroom would smell like jasmine for hours afterwards), but it still wouldn't make me desirable. Or at least not to them, the men who see a young woman in their bed as a status symbol. Women like me were a bad omen. We represented change.

The moth was long dead. I wasn't worried about him. Tomorrow, I'd be able to get on the bus again. I could go to the park, or the supermarket, or order a coffee in a café, and no one would be able to see that I'd been defiled. My clothing had been washed, and my boots were new. I had a roof over my head and a passport. My age rendered me a trustworthy woman. At cafés, strangers were likely to ask me if I could look after their laptop while they took a stroll. Young mothers would smile at me when I looked at their babies. If I wanted to, I could thoroughly blend into the crowd. Their judgement would never find me.

I leaned over the kitchen counter and thought about the promise of lip gloss and pink Hello Kitty sneakers. How easy it is to be attractive when you are young, the currency you have. Your desires aren't yet seen as ridiculous, and your experiences aren't mocked. Sitting on fresh sheets, you daydream about all your possible futures and ruminate about superficial matters. You are the kind of audience movie theatres are desperate to attract, and yet, you're entirely unaware of it. You work at a call centre and are saving up for a nose job. If you speak in metaphors, people are automatically impressed by you. You're given wristbands in clubs to show that you're underage. And death is just a concept to you.

To a certain extent, I understand why older men want to sleep with girls. I also understand why some older women wish to be a girl again.

By the time the sun came up, I'd convinced myself of my innocence and was back to feeling invincible.

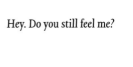

Hey. Do you still feel me?

SOMEONE IS TYPING A COMMENT...

It was supposed to feel like summer, but it was raining. All of us – we, the park visitors – had trusted the weather forecast, but it had betrayed us, and now our freshly coiffed hairstyles were perishing in front of our eyes. I took shelter beneath a tree. It helped for a bit.

There were clusters and pairs of people standing underneath other trees. Some of them had dogs. The dogs didn't give a shit about the rain and danced across the grass with frisbees in their mouths. The trees were resilient and protective, but it was raining so hard that within ten minutes, even they couldn't keep the rain at bay, and the water started gushing down the branches toward us.

It would take me thirty minutes to walk home. It was raining heavily, and I had to consider my options. There was an advertisement inside the bus shelter. It was a poster showing a young woman wearing lots of eyeliner and holding a glass ball. She was trying to sell perfume. I wasn't her target audience; I didn't possess the kind of *decadence* and *allure* that the perfume brand ascribed to themselves. Pedestrians and commuters were all around me. Who amongst these people, I wondered, would find the woman with the glass ball appealing? How many of them were brimming with decadence and allure?

Not one!

If I had been a successful photographer, there's no doubt I would have contributed to this very public kind of deception. I too, would have taken photographs based on arbitrary words to evoke people's desire for luxury. *Elegance. Sensuality.* In this version of reality, I would have directed a girl who was barely old enough to own real estate to gaze into the lens and look as sultry as possible, mouth open so her lips looked fuller. Post-production would take care of the rest – the perfect amount of innocence and the perfect amount of paedophilia. There would be controversy, but no lawsuit. And the perfume the image was advertising would be a popular Christmas present.

Everyone on the bus was longing for dressing gowns and takeaway dinners. Fantasies of ordinary weekends hung in the aisle. At least half of these people would fall asleep spooning with another body that night. I tightly gripped the rubber handle that hung from the ceiling and thought of nothing.

For a moment, it seemed like everything was forgivable.

At home, I discovered that I'd left the window open again. The windowsill was wet, and my ceramic pelicans were damp, as if they'd been crying their eyes out while I was away. And the wind had rattled my blinds so loudly that the neighbours who lived directly beside me had come to complain as soon as they heard me unlocking the front door.

Hey. Do you still feel me?

But nothing had been forgiven.

A green light flashed on my phone, not because someone was longing for my presence but because I'd overlooked an email in my inbox. It was a message from the website, or the website's moderator, to be precise. He reminded me that I hadn't opened the email concerning my banishment from the site. There was, he wrote, still some controversy regarding my contribution to the 'Girls' sub-forum and it had been reported to the police via an online helpdesk. The disgusting, terrible thing that I had done hadn't been forgotten.

All of this wasn't something I wanted to be updated on. I poured myself a glass of water but didn't take a sip. Instead, I counted the forks in my cutlery drawer. It was the only kind of mindfulness I would permit myself. I considered dropping my phone into the glass of water.

Think of the coast in summer… Think about sunlight and ice cream… Definitely don't think about dead kittens… Remember the good things from your childhood.

I despised every plane in the sky.

A strong smell rolled into my kitchen. It was the scent of summer and death. My neighbours had fired up their barbecue. I could smell their sausages and meat patties through the open window. Maybe they were throwing a party. The hypocrisy! Complaining about the vocal range of my blinds, only to pollute the air with their burning meat!

Young lady, this is your final warning. If you don't look at this now, we'll come and get you.

What kind of meat were my neighbours serving anyway? What were the sausages and meat patties made from? In an apartment complex like this, where everyone keeps to themselves, could you throw a pet on the barbecue without anyone knowing?

They could even be roasting children, their very own children, babies younger than two years old. If people could put puppies in garbage bags or leave a nest of kittens to the rats, then I suppose they could barbecue a baby every now and then.

This is how I convinced myself my neighbours were evil people.

I looked at my bright purple boots, which I'd parked next to the front door. At least you guys are honest, I told them. You're distinctive and, at the same time, quite simple. You aren't the kind of shoes to lead a secret double life. Straight-to-the-point, that's what you are. So different from my neighbours, those cannibals!

With a pounding heart, I closed the kitchen window, but my actions had absolutely no effect – the murderous fumes wouldn't dissipate.

I let my phone slip into the glass of water. The screen was too wide, the phone wouldn't drown. The glass of water fell over, creating a puddle on my floor and I swore.

That pelican, the one that always made the rattling sound, would know what to do. It was, after all, an extraordinary pelican. Not only that, but he also carried a gift in his hollow belly. Yes, the pelican held the Key to my Black Box. If I asked him nicely, he would surely give me the answers the fortune teller had kept from me on my birthday. He would be able to save me from what was to come.

But after all those years of sitting on the windowsill, the pelican still had to be convinced. Look at those wet cheeks – the animal was utterly distraught because he'd been neglected! I had to comfort him immediately, so that he could comfort me afterwards.

Dear Pelican, I began, I've known you for such a long time, you have to help me. No, don't cry, I've already closed the window. Let's dry your tears. Wait, I have a tea towel. There, that's better. So, can you help me?

The pelican cleared his throat before he spoke. He'd been silent for almost twenty years. He needed to warm up, like a cabaret singer or a raclette grill. When he finally opened his beak, he sounded small but noble.

How can I help, dear Thistle?

Oh, thank god, you're eager to listen. Do you smell that, Pelican? The window is closed, but I can still smell war. They're running a butcher shop right next door. And children's bodies are bearing the brunt of it. People need to eat, and the neighbours seem to have taken that to heart! What on earth should we do?

Calm down, I have the Key! I'm the pelican, and you're the woman who lives in this apartment. You're thirty-three years old, and you sleep alone. And for whatever sketchy reason, you like taking pictures of underage kids. If it weren't for your dead father, you'd be homeless. You wear boots that make you look like a cartoon character – a somewhat alluring cartoon character, let me be clear about that – and you have the longest neck I've ever seen on an adult woman. You're an outsider, a nutcase, but there's strength to be found in your incompetence, so use it!

Okay, okay. Should I show my face at the neighbours' house? Should I knock at their door and complain very loudly?

No, no, no, that would be asking for trouble and humiliation! You must do the opposite. You need to hide. Truly, profoundly hide yourself. You should hide from your neighbours here, in your very own house.

How can I truly, profoundly hide myself? What would that look like?

You'll have to wait and see.

And then, if you can imagine it, the pelican hurled himself against the wall. There was nothing left of him. He was smashed to smithereens. There's nothing left of my father except my eyes, I thought. My eyes, my eyes that rarely get to experience anything truly precious!

I rummaged through the remaining shards of the pelican, searching for the thing inside of him, but found nothing, just more shards. It was still raining. The water streamed swiftly down my windows and told me to *stay inside, stay inside.*

Just when I thought it wasn't possible to find anyone else to talk to, the hallway closet flew open, and five familiar faces tumbled into my living room – the weasels. I hadn't seen them since I'd moved out of the family home, but that didn't seem to bother these creatures. They made themselves at home, just as they used to. They looked around, sniffed at all my belongings, bared their teeth and crept under my covers with dubious looks on their faces. That too!

I let out a shriek. I shrieked for a long time.

Hey. Do you still feel me?

The doorbell rang. It was the postal service. They had a package for me that was too big to fit through my letterbox. There was no way I was going to accept a package in person during a war. I told the postman he could leave the package at the entrance to the stairwell, and everyone was happy with that solution (the postman, the package, and me).

I felt terribly scared as I made my way downstairs, but not because of my neighbours. I was scared because I was naked. Luckily, there was no one else in the stairwell. My package was lying in the lobby like an outcast. Once I was back inside my apartment, I noticed I could no longer smell death and destruction. My neighbours had ceased their barbecuing.

What is the prototype for an ordinary life? Don't fall, don't get sick, don't flip out – the usual suspects. Just those garden-variety fears that every happy person has.

Don't say anything crazy at a party. That's absolutely not done!

Don't eat with your mouth full. The rest of the group will be disgusted!

Don't bring up uncomfortable topics at an otherwise comfortable and stupidly pleasant event!

If the people around you flee from an incident, then you should also flee. Think about your position within the group!

In an emergency, always shout 'fire' and never 'help' because people don't listen to the latter! No one wants to be drawn into an uncomfortable situation.

Don't romanticise your own demise!

Don't masturbate over photos of underage people!

And: never, ever, ever choose the past over the urgency of today!

The package contained a large piece of reflective fabric, which transformed into light whenever it was photographed. If I wore this while shooting a self-portrait, the camera's light would capture a white flare instead of my body. Just my head would be visible, the only piece of my person that I could afford to expose. The reflective cloth would also make it impossible for all the bad people to find me, and as long as I couldn't be found, I wouldn't be victimised.

Unfortunately, I forgot that I was also a bad person and my head, cruel as it was, could outsmart the light!

Beanbag would say that I was unhealthily obsessed with offsetting the loss I'd experienced as a child. That I was seeking approval in all the wrong place because I had never learnt the right places to seek it. And from this, it was clear that I hadn't properly processed my grief. A more expensive therapist might say that I was compulsively recreating the original circumstances that caused my fears but hoping for a better outcome. And that I was trying to control the narrative by choosing my own defect: it's better to be the woman with the dirty photos than the girl with the dead father. *You're overcompensating*, this therapist would say, and I'd accept the box of tissues she'd subtly push my way.

And a random narcissist would have bundled up the whole mess, put it in a file labelled 'Inspiration' and used it as material for their artistic career (till death did them part).

Why did the man have to die such a ridiculous death? My father, the man who taught me how to do long division. Every time someone asked about his death, I felt as if they were making a fool of me. It was like being forced to walk along the street carrying a family-sized pack of toilet paper. It's normal to laugh when confronted with death. My mother and I once laughed when we heard that someone we knew had been diagnosed with breast cancer.

There were files on my desktop containing all the photos I'd ever taken that I thought were worth saving. During my course, I'd even photographed a wedding. The resulting images became the blueprint for 'a good family', with every conceivable role represented. There were smiling fathers and mothers, grandparents helping to distribute pieces of wedding cake, bridesmaids screeching and mustering like animals of prey.

The only moment of doubt was when they were all told they had to jump for the camera, at which point all those faces – happy, smiling faces – suddenly morphed into artifacts of primitive exertion. During the jump, all their tensions revealed themselves. The mother-in-law's doubts and the best friend's jealousy. The discomfort of the plus-ones, who hadn't known the family long enough to justify their presence, like the guy with the ludicrous bow tie at the back of the group who would cry himself to sleep that night because he was single and lonely.

After I completed the course, I was never asked to photograph another wedding again, and my private life was similarly devoid of wedding cakes. I had once taken staff photographs for a yoga studio. Three instructors, all women, smiled as they touched their toes without bending their knees. I put all their headshots and other poses into separate files. Ultimately, they'd only wanted the headshots, because they were too vain to appreciate the action shots I'd taken. These photos revealed their bodies doing things that weren't quite as controlled as they'd hoped. There were wrinkles on their foreheads, and the skin on their shoulders was saggy.

There was also that photo of the girl, the toddler I'd documented at the fountain that day, before I'd lost control of myself and the tick found its way to my neck. The girl wasn't filed away; she was saved on my desktop, just as I'd planned.

And then there were the photos of my baby niece, the unauthorised photos that had ruined my second chance at a relationship with my Sister.

I wouldn't stand a chance in a courtroom, that much was certain.

The weasels in my bed were singing a foreboding song. I couldn't understand their language, but that is precisely what made their song so foreboding.

One of the yoga photos showed the instructors on their knees. Their upper bodies were bent over so far that their foreheads touched the mats. Their arms were stretched out in front of them with their palms flat on the ground. This pose, they told me, was called the 'child's pose'.

I lay my head on the floor and mimicked the pose, then slept for the first time in thirty-five hours.

A clock without hands hanging on the wall. An unforgiving fluorescent light above my head. And me, aborting a child that had already been born.

A nurse put an ice cube in a face cloth and placed it on my forehead. A doctor asked what I was working on. A perfume ad, I answered.

Is that tax-deductible? she asked.

The child didn't cry when it was removed.

I'd like to have something to drink, I said.

The nurse emptied the contents of the face cloth into my mouth. The melted ice tasted like hibiscus.

Gentrification, the doctor declared while shaking her head.

Where is my child? I asked the big light on the ceiling that shone only on my head.

On the upstairs neighbours' barbecue, said the doctor.

In the package at the bottom of the stairs, said the assistant.

In the pelican's belly, said Beanbag, who was standing in the doorway.

You're all useless, I said witheringly.

And shortly after this, I woke up with a headache.

The afternoon was quiet, damp, and surreal. I looked at the ceiling and imagined the soles of my upstairs neighbours' feet. How did the inventor of the microscope feel when he discovered all that was invisible to the naked eye? Whatever that feeling was, I must have come very close to it.

I washed the anxious sweat out of my hair in the shower. The scent of my shampoo recalled a pine forest, full of young wolves sleeping in the hollows. I shut my eyes, let the water stream down my cheeks and visualised the powdered sugar on their noses – powdered sugar made of fresh snow, of winter sports. Somewhere, someone is on holiday, I thought, and that someone will soon be completely relaxed...

The water wouldn't drain. My feet were immersed in the warmth, and the water was turbid from the soap and my filth. That was all I needed! Was there something stuck in the drain? The weasels, I thought initially, they've sabotaged my only moment of relaxation because they're such inherently hateful beasts!

One glance around the living room debunked that theory: the weasels had left my duvet and were now hanging in my curtains. They had heedless looks on their faces, insofar as weasels are able to assume such an expression. They had other plans for me, the kind of plans that required an overview and no moments of relaxation; oh no, they required utter vigilance.

A quick field assessment revealed that all my belongings were still intact. The weasels hadn't employed them as tools for my destruction—at least, not yet. The distress signal I was searching for had failed to materialise. I slithered back to the shower on my wet feet. In the meantime, the water had risen quite high. The weasels! Maybe they hadn't jammed the drain with something I owned, but instead used one of themselves, the furry corpse of a sacrificed brother… The fortune teller had said something about an animal. Was a dead weasel my life companion? I feared the fungus that was bound to follow this kind of water damage.

It was an afternoon that demanded courage. My house was full of unhuman eyes, I had no clothes on my body, and there was untold evil hiding in the most intimate room…

I didn't do it willingly, but my hand was decisive, my hand was brave, my hand had done far worse things.

Reaching into the drain, I pulled out a clump of hair. Blonde hairs, far lighter than my own and also much longer. Who or what had been using my shower? Was this nasty tangle the legacy of a previous owner or an uninvited guest? It had been almost fifteen years since I'd signed the transfer deed…

The clump of hairs felt like a valuable asset. It was a significant acquisition, a treasure I'd dug up from my bathroom's secret bowels… The hair was wet from years of shower water and smelt familiar. Yes, there was no question it belonged to me. On which part of me had it grown? Had it sprouted from the part that was tiny, fuzzy and immature, the part of me that up until recently had been cared for by the ceramic pelican?

How shameless I was! Still naked and clutching the clump of hair against my chest. I took the time to consider my options. For my entire adult life, up until now, I'd been fascinated by the pelican bequeathed to me – but why? That phony-beaked fraud! With a body that rattled but turned out to be empty, and zero depth behind the pelican's mysterious façade… What an empty, empty existence it must be when there's no possibility of going any deeper. Perhaps I could find some way to make up for the loss. Yes, I, too, could put something in my belly that didn't belong.

It happened before I could stop myself: I stuck the clump of hair in my mouth, then swallowed it. Once it was in my throat, the link to the sewer seemed clearer; suddenly, I was smelling perversities I hadn't smelt before. I was polluting myself, perhaps even poisoning myself with a clump of someone else's past. Why did I do such things?

I regretted not photographing the hairs before I swallowed them. The combination of taste and texture, the unknown elements from the sewer, and all the mealy threads that were stuck in my oesophagus… I was making myself sick!

Retching has never been a strength of mine. I'll admit that in the past, I might have shoved a spoon or two down my throat while attempting to lose a kilo or two, but I didn't have the willpower to actually destroy my body. I was constantly eating pastries and soaking in the bath, and these kinds of things don't go hand in hand with destruction. I permitted myself both beauty and comfort. Before going to bed, I've always massaged my cheeks with moisturising cream. When I turned eighteen, my first purchase was the most comprehensive dental insurance that money could buy. I wanted to be the girl in the spotlight, alluring and eye-catching while still being part of the herd. I wanted to be special but not deviate from the norm, and despite my superiority, I wanted to be saved by others. I wouldn't perish in the claws of a hunter. The trick to hunting is to isolate the prey… but I refused to be isolated!

If I was prey, how would I taste?

This is something I could have asked my blood relatives, if I had them.

That afternoon by the fountain, I found myself in another world – and now it was happening again.

The light in the apartment changed. I could hear the water streaming through my pipes and the material under my base-boards cracking. My walls turned to flesh. My thoughts were amplified, and an unfamiliar voice bubbled up inside my head.

The words were unclear. They sounded as if they were being spoken by someone who was hanging underneath the tap, as if they were trying to drink from the tap and talk at the same time. It took me a moment to get used to it, almost as if it were an accent. I had to adjust until I grasped their style of speaking. The voice was authoritative, angular. After a short while, I could understand it:

Hey. Do you still feel me?

Where am I supposed to feel you?

In the lump on your neck.

The tick! I thought you were gone.

Instinctively, I put my hand on the place he described. The tiny lump was no longer there. My body had healed itself.

I can't feel you under my skin, I said. I didn't know you were still with me.

I suspected as much, sighed the tick. *I know exactly what you've done.*

They were my photos. It was my own body.

Your audience doesn't care about that. And neither do the police. I think they're building a case against you.

You're trying to scare me. You managed to sneak in here on the coat of one of the weasels, right? Is this some kind of power trip? You're like a barking dog. I know a threat when I hear one.

If you say so.

Why have you come back?

To reiterate, I've been keeping an eye on you. I never left. But now I'm speaking up because it's time.

For what?

Things are about to change.

A lot has changed already. I barely recognise my own apartment. My computer is gone. Strangers have taken over my phone. Inanimate things I've owned for years have suddenly started speaking. And now you. Now you've started speaking too!

That's right.

I ate a hairball earlier. I've never eaten a hairball before.

That's enough recapping for now, thank you. We have to get on with it. The clock is ticking.

Do you exist outside of my mind?

Of course I exist. I'm made of blood, just like you.

Then where are you? The physical form of you, not just your voice. I'm curious to see if your teeth are just as sharp in real life as they are in my head.

I'm in the hall. Just open the front door.

Wait a second, I'm naked! I can't open the door like this. What would my neighbours think? You can be sure that they'll just happen to be in the hall if I go out there like this. Just a moment, I'll put on some clothes. Hmmm, what should I wear? It needs to be something discreet.

You have that reflective cloth, remember? Just put that on, it looks good on you. Yes, I was watching when you opened that package. I saw the way you stood triumphantly in front of the mirror. I told you I've been keeping an eye on you. And none of your neighbours are home. Your next-door neighbours and upstairs neighbours have gone out hunting for fresh meat. They've already eaten all the meat they had. Quick, come outside! Believe me, the coast is clear.

Yes, okay… Okay, okay, okay. The coast is clear, you say. Well, I'm coming. Where are my boots? I don't want to go out there with bare feet; I've done that once today. And once per day is my maximum when it comes to going barefoot.

As long as you hurry up. I'll be waiting in the stairwell.

The weasels in the curtains hissed at me viciously. Their planned coup was about to be thwarted by some mystical fate, and they could smell it. I couldn't stand the way they looked at me and put my boots on as quickly as I could. In my hurry, I pulled up the zip too roughly, and it caught my skin. The pain made me wince, but I didn't want to give the weasels the satisfaction of seeing another dent in my armour. Feigning calm, I grabbed the reflective cloth off the floor and wrapped it around me as if it were a toga. Indeed, it looked good on me, but the material was poor quality and made my armpits itch. My boots said tk, tk, tk when I stepped over the threshold.

The tick was right: there was no one in the hall. Relieved, I strode over to the stairwell.

Ah, there you are.

Yes, here I am. But I don't see you. Where should I look?

Let's worry about that later. Quick, come with me. We must go upstairs.

Has the moth returned?

The moth? No, there aren't any moths here.

That's a shame.

Come upstairs now. Quick.

Yeah, yeah, yeah. I can't move any faster in this garment. And my boots feel heavy. So, so heavy. Why aren't we taking the lift?

Stop moaning. You're almost there.

What have you got up there anyway? It's not a surprise party, is it? I hate surprise parties.

Just trust me.

That was easier said than done. It isn't easy to trust a situation when you're climbing stairs in a toga while following a voice that only exists in your head.

The tick had lied about being in the stairwell, that creature was nowhere to be found. I'd walked up those stairs all alone, obedient as a dog. Now, I was standing – practically naked – in front of my neighbours' door. The light on the landing switched on: my presence had been registered, even if I knew it was only temporary. If I were to do nothing, the light would switch off again. If I didn't move, the darkness would return to me. But was that what I wanted? No, I didn't want the darkness – I wanted sunlight and serenity. If I had to die of something, then for heaven's sake, please let it be sunlight and serenity.

I had to move quickly, just as the tick had urged – I had to be quick before the darkness returned!

Tick, what exactly is the plan here? I don't see you, and I don't know what I'm supposed to be doing.

Come closer.

Closer to where? The window?

Nonono, the shoe cabinet of course.

Oh! The shoe cabinet. Of course, I need some other shoes. A new phase of life requires new shoes. Because that's what's about to happen, right? A big change.

Indeed.

I'm going to become a different person again. And these boots don't suit the new me. No, these boots are unsuitable for the future. They're way too flashy. I must learn how to present a more nuanced version of myself.

Now that you mention it, I was wondering why you'd spent your money on those things.

They made me think of pop stars and technology.

Women your age wear black, white or gold. Any other colour is an assault on your credibility.

Why should anyone believe me at all? I'm not a good woman.

Take a look in the cabinet. Is there something for you in there? I see some mules on the top shelf. They're quite ladylike, don't you think?

Well, those aren't really my taste. I don't know how to wear shoes that don't have any heel support, I'd probably trip over them. But look at these sneakers, they're not so bad. They don't stink, and they look quite comfortable.

You're a strange one. Have you considered asking them if you are to their taste? You can't just assume that every shoe wants you, Thistle. That kind of overconfidence won't win you any friends.

Huh? Oh, yes, you're right, of course. I got ahead of myself. Sorry, a thousand apologies. Dear sneakers, am I to your liking?

…

What size are you?

…

Hello? Hello?

…

How do you know the tick?

…

Hey Tick! How am I supposed to know if they want me?

A door opened – it was my upstairs neighbours' front door and my upstairs neighbour stood on the threshold. Clearly not out on the hunt, she was wearing a facial mask that smelled like avocado. It was the type of mask that people put on when they're trying to force themselves to relax. My neighbour's head represented wellness, well-being, and the colour green. My shock at the sight of her was quite brutal, so much so that I dropped the reflective cloth I was holding, and for a moment, just a moment, I was completely naked.

The air of manufactured relaxation dissipated on the spot. Cracks appeared in the green crust covering my neighbour's forehead, suggesting that she'd spent her younger years frowning, and the social repercussions of this were now unavoidable.

Stammering, I tried to explain that I had a guest (an invisible guest, admittedly, but a guest nonetheless) who was looking for new shoes and thought they might find them here, upstairs, but my visitor had underestimated how busy it would be on the landing. And apart from that, all my decent clothing had been taken over by a horde of weasels who'd appeared in my living room out of nowhere and were apparently no longer willing to vacate my space. I told her in detail about the weasels hanging in my curtains and how they were sitting in their watchtower looking down and judging me. Then, I tried to involve my neighbour in my current situation, my meeting with the future. Yes, I did my absolute best to impress upon her the fleeting nature of the present. But my neighbour's priorities lay elsewhere.

What in god's name are you doing with my shoes? she asked.

CHLOË SEVIGNY ISN'T
LOOKING AT THE CAMERA

They would call it a lapse of moral judgement if I were to follow every one of their orders; a sex crime if I refused to cooperate. I dressed myself in proper clothing before they took me away because they didn't find my mirrored toga acceptable attire. And all throughout, the weasels had remained in my apartment, criticising me with their eyes, but it didn't bother me anymore because I had more pressing problems to deal with. I did everything they asked of me and risked my own life getting dressed while surrounded by the weasels.

When they wanted to make a copy of my passport, I said yes. When they asked for my phone, I gave it to them. I've forgotten all the other things they asked of me.

Your memory is like a sieve, my mother had said right before she kicked me out of home. I wish I was as good at forgetting things as you are.

According to the officer, there were certain factors that would determine how I was to be *convicted* and *sentenced*.

I'd chosen a polo-neck jumper and jeans, which was my fixed uniform for ordinary days. Truly, I hoped that if I did everything expected of me, it would turn out to be an ordinary day, without any particular future in sight. I surprised myself with this thought. Didn't I want to turn into a person in the spotlight? Where was my ambition?

There was no time to be disappointed. Once again, I had to make haste, take the lift down to the ground floor and get into a car. Once I was in the lift, I quickly checked my teeth. They were gleaming, thank god, and my gums were nice and pink. There was absolutely no evidence that I'd just eaten some hair, which was good because it meant they had nothing on me and couldn't lock me up.

I was brought into the police station with my wrists behind my back. As soon as I arrived, I was told to take off my boots. And that reassured me, because it felt almost familiar, as if I was visiting a friend's house instead of being arrested. The posse of police officers felt celebratory, and for a moment, I dared to hope I'd be offered a drink to welcome me, but nothing like that happened. It quickly became apparent that this visit was strictly business.

My boots disappeared into a plastic container. I also had to give up my keys. They disappeared into the fist of one of my jailors. The police officers – at least I think they were police officers – let me sit in a waiting room until I could feel my bones. My bum also protested, but I didn't listen to its complaints. I wouldn't let myself be intimidated any longer.

I was alone in the waiting room. The door was locked. A security camera was keeping a close eye on me. I looked into the lens and forgot all about the vulnerability of my situation. The camera, my old friend! – I'd accidentally become the punchline to my own joke.

It was fifteen minutes or so before the waiting room door opened. To my delight, I was given a meal, but it wasn't a particularly inspiring meal. There was a sandwich consisting of two (2) slices of bread and a thick slab of cheese. Under the cheese, I discovered a substantial layer of butter that had been carelessly spread across the bread. I was amazed by the sheer amount of dairy. People who live in cities generally don't eat sandwiches. Instead, we eat curries, noodles and smoothies, and, if we find ourselves in the company of others, we like to eat mezze.

I took a bite of the sandwich and could immediately taste that the bread had been in the freezer. It tasted cold and spongy. There was nothing erotic about it. That poor battered bread! I covered the sandwich with my serviette. It looked so forlorn I couldn't bring myself to eat it. I'd accept the stomach pain I was sure to get from it with compassion.

Another fifteen minutes later, I was taken from the waiting room. I was led, in my socks, to a small office referred to as the 'conference room'. And in this room, the officers asked me a series of questions. Were the photos on the forum mine? If so, could I prove it? Why had I posted them online? Had I received any financial compensation for the photos? And if not, had I done it with the intention of receiving financial compensation? Did I have children? Was I in a relationship? Was I working in education or healthcare? Had the photos been circulated outside the forum, or was it the only place they could be found online?

Their second question was the most challenging for me to answer. The current me looked nothing like the girl I was sixteen years ago. The doubt playing at the corners of my mouth had disappeared, my eyes were quite different now, and yes, my body had grown heavier. For a moment, I envied my Sister. Why hadn't I been the one to get a butterfly tattoo? Why hadn't I gotten any kind of tattoo when our father died? I hadn't demanded any photos of him after the funeral. I hadn't taken any of his clothes from the wardrobe to preserve his scent. I hadn't done anything to immortalise my father.

Or rather, I hadn't done anything that would be considered appropriate.

I tried to defend myself.

Have you seen the length of my neck? (I pointed at my throat.) You could already see the beginnings of it back then. Look at the first photo! And my overbite, I had it then too. (I bit the air to demonstrate.) I never got it fixed. Braces are far too expensive, and apart from that, I can't deal with any kind of pain in my mouth. I don't have any cavities. In fact, I have outstanding dental insurance. Oh, and do you see those breasts? They're like pointy egg yolks, an unimpressive pair. (I pulled up my jumper.) The skin around them isn't as smooth as it once was, but their shape is more or less the same. (At their request, I pulled down my sweater again.) Hmmm, what else... Oh, how could I forget? The lines on my hands, you really should read those. Literally anything you could ever want to know about me is written on my hands. The last person I consulted only had bad news for me, so I've recently been searching for a second opinion. Yes, I'm taking a *proactive* approach to my recovery.

I attempted to lean back in the uncomfortable chair. Then, I crossed my legs. My defence was successful, I thought; the opposition wouldn't be able to come up with a response. That is, until I saw the underside of my socks. All the wandering around without shoes on had turned the soles of socks black. It was a bad omen. I was disappointed once again, and I missed my boots, which would surely have offered me some protection from all that filth.

While I was worrying about this and that, the officers got down to business. They weren't particularly interested in the lines on my hand, more so in my fingerprints. No, they didn't recognise me in the body of that seventeen-year-old girl. Yes, they had doubts about my story and general persona. Even though I really hoped it would be different.

They let me stay a little longer.

My poor, purple boots. Lonely and alone in a plastic container. Well, perhaps not lonely – they still had each other, thank god. In that respect, they were better off than I, who'd been brought back to the waiting room to wait for an unspecified amount of time.

I was given a magazine to pass the time. And guess what? I'm not making this up… That photo of Chloë Sevigny was on the cover! It was the same photo I'd seen at the shoe shop just a few days prior. Had she died or something? Is that why she was suddenly so popular? The films she appeared in were generally quite intense; she didn't have the kind of oeuvre that appealed to all and sundry… Why would she even be part of a shop display?

The magazine didn't offer me any answers. There was an interview with the photographers who had taken the photo, because there was going to be an exhibition of their work at the national museum. The magazine also mentioned that the photo of Sevigny would be part of the exhibition. It was one of their earlier works. Indeed, that photo was more than twenty years old. The dates for the exhibition were listed at the bottom of the article. You could see it up until... last summer. What was I supposed to do with that? – The reading material in the waiting room wasn't current. I felt duped, betrayed, ticked off. The officers were just as bad as the weasels in my apartment, they'd conspired and hatched an evil plan against me. They wanted me to lose track of time!

I threw the magazine on the floor. The pages flipped open, making a beautiful sound as the magazine landed. I went to sit next to it and tore the pages into strips so I could listen to that sound again. Tssk, tssk, tssk. The perfume ads all perished, one by one. Even Sevigny had to suffer. The cover of the magazine was too thick to rip into neat strips, so I turned it into little snowflakes.

After half an hour the magazine was no more. The tearing noises had been so relaxing that I'd completely forgotten about the security camera. Still, no one had interrupted my destruction of the magazine, so my behaviour, I concluded, was forgivable. I surveyed my work and was pleased.

The tearing orchestra made way for a less welcome sound. In the left corner of the waiting room was a radiator that started rattling just as I had destroyed the magazine's last summer tip (scrub your skin before sun exposure, not after!). I had a worrying conversation with that radiator. He knew only one human word, and he constantly repeated it. Run, run, run – the refrain of a desperate beast. The poor thing had gone crazy, that much was clear. And it was entirely possible that this would also be my fate, because I'd been alone for far too long. People who are alone for too long are defenceless against the unknown. They see even the smallest change as a threat. It renders them permeable. It's bad shit!

I found myself in bad company. The poor radiator, he was obviously erratic... Who would come and save me from this conversation? Had the tick already heard of my arrest? Would he come and pick me up as soon as I was allowed to leave? Would he ever appear outside of my head at all? I longed for blood relatives.

As suddenly as he had opened his trap, the radiator fell silent again. He probably just needed to pour out his heart. I was no stranger to that concept, it happens more often in life: someone having an issue they need to get off their chest. And if I acquiesce and give the impression that I'm a willing listener, the wounded soul will usually burst open. I show them my warmth and my patience and anticipate the deep conversations that tend to follow this kind of confession. And after all that attention, the wounded soul is, huzzah, magically healed – and the owner of it will, once again, leave me to my own devices. Before I'm able to reveal anything of myself, before I even get the chance to make an impression with my own complex life stories, I find myself alone again. Overlooked, left behind and ignored by someone supposedly in the same boat.

And now that I think about it, that's exactly what the tick had done...

I gave the radiator a kick. It probably hurt me more than it hurt him, though the kick reverberated inside his chassis for an incredibly long time. And the sound of it brought me solace. It was the expression of every anguished shriek I'd never let those opportunists utter. I promised myself that from this moment on, it would be different. In the future, I wouldn't let myself be treated like dirt.

My loneliness stagnated. I felt stronger than before, even if I had to admit that the officers had gotten their way: I'd completely lost track of time. It must have been gradually getting dark outside. Or maybe a new morning had arrived. I hated the woman who lived upstairs! I wanted her to die in a ridiculous way – with her face covered in the green mask, she'd slip in her bathroom, and her last word would be something like 'Oops'. Her entire history of verbal communication would end in humiliation. The thought of this felt good, it made me laugh out loud. Oops, what a ridiculous word to send you six feet under!

I promised myself that as soon as my neighbour was buried, I'd choose a sunny day to seek out her final resting place. I'd be bursting with life, and I'd kick her headstone. I could totally picture it happening, accompanied by a video-game soundtrack and oh, oh, how it made me laugh.

The waiting room door opened.

Madam? You can follow me.

The person who asked me to follow them wasn't someone I'd seen before. There must have been a change of shift while I'd been in the waiting room, which meant that the person who'd brought me the sandwich was probably already sitting on the bus, on his way home, where a dressing gown and glass of milk would be waiting for him, perhaps even a loved one, and a television series that never ended…

I kept following in my socks. We walked down a hall, past a row of windows, which were covered on the inside by closed blinds. At the end of the hall was a small room with a red door which had a little hatch that could slide open. Inside the room was a bedframe, a rubber mattress and a sink with a tap you had to press a button on to operate. I was to remain here until 'further notice'. There had never been a crueller indication of time!

The room also had a security camera hanging on the wall. At the counter in the hall was a guard who would observe my behaviour in captivity. He told me I should 'give him a shout' if I needed anything. Because, he continued, the guard would creep out from behind the counter to come down and see what it was I was shouting about at that particular moment. After I'd finished complaining, they would find a fitting solution. Then, whatever was amiss would be peacefully rectified.

If I had to wee, the guard said, then I should also 'give him a shout', and when he said that to me, I had to laugh again, because it reminded me of my neighbour. Everyone who was present frowned when I did that, and just like that, I was one point behind on the scoreboard of their collective view.

Before the tiny sliding window in the door closed, I asked if I could have a pen and paper, but that wasn't permitted: a pen is a potential weapon. I wasn't even allowed a *pencil and paper*. This really surprised me, because I thought the softer tip and general informality of a pencil would make it less controversial, but oh no, potential murder weapons like pencils were clearly out of the question.

After a series of pathetic sighs from my end, the guard returned with a notebook and a wax crayon. It was the kind of thing you're given in nursery school when you say you want to 'draw' something. The crayon was dark blue and smelt like wet earth. I was really pleased with it and immediately put it to work! Despite the paper's rough texture, the blue easily slid over the page. I used my thighs as an easel, just like bohemians in films. Artistic women in American films, French films – in all films.

I drew an enormous sneaker with tied laces. No particular brand, so there was no need to draw a logo on its flank. It was big enough to fit a Sinterklaas present. Yes, I could cut the best sneaker from a piece of paper, put it in a random shoe cabinet and then all I'd have to do was wait until December, when Sinterklaas would come and start filling everyone's shoes with gifts. Or! I could put a present in there myself. Some unknown recipient could discover it, and who knows, maybe they'd be utterly delighted by such an unexpected gift. There were so many lovely potential futures. I smiled the entire length of the sneaker, up until I'd finished drawing – see, there! Now my captivity could continue in peace.

The guard was interested in my work. He'd been following my progress on the monitor attached to the security camera, and now I was looking straight ahead, and appeared satisfied. He knew the moment had arrived: my drawing was complete. Under the pretext of a routine check-in, he questioned me through the sliding window. What exactly, he asked, had I made?

I responded with a mysterious smile. This guard probably thought I was some kind of famous artist and that this drawing – which I had done under his supervision, no less! – was worth some money. Loads of money. Of course, I'd have to disappoint him, but for a moment – a short moment – the suggestion of hope hung in the air.

The drawing was examined while I studied the face of the guard. He was more expressive than I'd initially thought. I saw his hopeful expression move to doubt and then change again into something different, all too familiar disappointment or, no… offense!

Indeed, the guard was offended. He tore my blue sneaker to shreds.

Don't draw dirty pictures, he said disapprovingly, and he made a little ball out of all the pieces of paper that were once my drawing. Then, the guard left my cell and shut the little window. Out of pure frustration, I gave him a shout.

And that's how my residency in the holding cell came to an end. Those perpetually anonymous officers returned and told me I was to sleep somewhere else that night.

Where that 'somewhere' would be wasn't specified. In my current state, both time and place were kept from me. Despite all this, I still did what I was told, following the officers out of the room and into a cloakroom, where my purple boots were already waiting, wagging their tails in their container. I put them on and stroked the spot where the metal zip turned into leather.

Ahhh…

I immediately forgot that the zip had screwed me over earlier that day.

Hurry up, said the officers. The driver isn't a fan of waiting.

It was windy in the parking lot. I was only briefly outside, but there were still goosebumps underneath my sleeves. I hadn't brought a jacket with me, and I was wearing my jeans, a polo neck jumper, and nothing else, apart from my dirty socks and a general air of displacement. Only once I'd fastened my seatbelt did I understand my 'somewhere' was in a completely different building. Perhaps it was even in an entirely different city – or another world!

There was a young guy wearing a pair of white overalls beside me in the car. I wondered what he (young and not ugly) had done to get himself in this position. If he was a sex offender, I didn't think it was right of them to put him next to me, a woman! But my judgement rapidly evaporated once I realised that I had also been booked as a sex offender.

The car windows were heavily tinted. I couldn't see any further than the road directly beside me and I found that unsettling. I was used to looking at the horizon, counting the birds and seeing all the cyclists. Now all I could see were the white stripes on the asphalt and the brightest of streetlights, which shone straight through the tinted windows. I missed all the buildings that passed us, the tops of the trees and the freedom of my usual routine.

I compensated by succumbing to an old nervous habit: I bit my fingernails, and they tasted like pavement chalk.

Aren't we feeding you enough? Is what my father would have bellowed if he were still alive.

The guy in the white overalls was stoic. He didn't say a word. He didn't look back at me once, even when I stared at him shamelessly. I could project whatever I wanted onto him. We turned a corner, a streetlight lit up his face temporarily, and it made me think about that song by The Smiths I used to like listening to when I cried, 'There Is a Light That Never Goes Out'.

It was a romantic number about unrequited love. The lyrics tell the story of two people sitting in a car. One of them is driving while the other sits in the passenger seat. The person sitting in the passenger seat is in love with the driver, but the driver… doesn't know it. The passenger fantasises about this being the evening in which he finally declares his love to the driver, after which the two head off into a long and sweet life together, full of good music and loads of long walks. But if that kind of future isn't what's in store for them, then the passenger is happy to settle for them both getting run over. Crashing a car together is also romantic – or at least it is more romantic than crashing a car on your own.

The first time I'd visited the online platform, in a sub-forum labelled 'Shocking', I'd seen a video of two men standing on the top floor of a burning building. The men had to choose between burning to death or falling to death from a great height, and they chose – after some panic – the latter. They embraced each other and jumped into the eternal loading screen together. A security camera had filmed the images. Shortly after the video was posted, it was taken offline again, because a moderator had said the content wasn't 'original' and was therefore in breach of the forum's regulations.

All the stoplights were conspiring against us. The chauffeur drove carefully, not wanting to risk a single orange light. It was a long drive, and I was nauseous from all the braking and accelerating but didn't dare complain: the air of authority in the car was so strong that no one dared to express any personal preferences. I rubbed my temples and prayed to the tick, who'd pretended to be my protector, but now that I really needed him, he was nowhere to be seen.

I was alone.

The indicator said *click-clack, click-clack*. We were slowing down. Could it be true? Had I in fact, as the route planner claimed, reached my destination?

When I stepped out of the car, I found myself standing in front of a familiar door. The apartment complex where I lived.

I was home.

'Somewhere' was my very own apartment, with my very own body inside it.

The guy in the white overalls followed me up the stairs. After the bumpy car ride, I'd thanked the driver for the lift. I couldn't handle any more G-force. I was delighted to hear the tk, tk, tk of my heels on the stairs. The guy stayed three steps behind me the entire time. He was wearing flat shoes, so his footsteps said nothing.

At the front door, my fears came back with a vengeance. What if the weasels were still in there…? What if the scent of culinary carcasses my neighbours had produced was still in the air…?

I didn't want to open the door.

And I couldn't open the door, because I didn't have the keys. The guy in the white overalls had them. He grinned as he magically made them appear and walked extra slowly, s-l-o-w-l-y, so I was forced to wait in front of my own door. The keys jingled in his hand.

Run, run, run, said the guy, before he opened my front door, turned on the light and gave me just ten minutes to pack my things.

There was a time when I was scared of getting lost, of pissing in the dark, of wearing pants with a fussy button, of standing on a chair on my birthday while everyone sang 'Happy Birthday' to me. There was a time when I was scared that I wouldn't find my calling, scared that I'd never menstruate, or never find true love and that I was ugly. Later, I became scared of becoming homeless, of filling in a form incorrectly and losing everything that mattered to me, of not hearing a car driving towards me, of finding a strange lump on my body and not knowing how I'd gotten it. Of hearing a loud bang, feeling a voice, tasting an image; and scared of experiencing time in a way that was radically different from every other present day.

And now? Now that all of this has happened, what do I still have to be scared of?

Death isn't going to come and get me. Life, on the other hand, is another story.

A BELL TOLLS IN THE DISTANCE,
BUT NOT FOR ME

There's a dark streak running the length of the ceiling. Water damage, poorly maintained. A few weeks ago, such a sight would have scared me, but it isn't a few weeks ago – it is the present, and in the present, my hands smell like green soap.

Hermit crab, implantation pain.

They say my grief is complex.

My earthly language has been lost. Now I only speak *clinimen.* It's a word I came up with to pass the time. It means: *the language used at the clinic.* I observe, I reflect, and I correct.

Ever since arriving here, I wake, eat and sleep at fixed times. The way I fill every hour of the day has been planned out in a roster, by people I've never met. All the spontaneity has been sucked out of my days; the randomness of real life doesn't stand a chance in here. Even the food they serve smells like nothing. I see a lot of wax crayons in my future.

My new home is located just beside a highway. You could say it's a somewhat dubious location for a building like this, but

I don't feel I'm in any danger. I need a special keycard to exit the building and nature itself lets me know what it is I have to fear.

Stay away from red berries!

I have my own room, but I'm only allowed to sleep in there. They say that it's good for me to be out 'amongst the people', which is why I am here observing, being observed.

The showers and toilets are shared. My sheets are changed once a week, but before this small pleasure is granted, I must first strip the bed of its dirty sheets myself, then throw them in a basket in the hall. I'm participating. I'm functioning.

Click-clack, click-clack.

The nursing staff all wear clogs.

During rush hour, one of the groups leaves the exercise room, the other group exits the 'drama room' and the people on the morning shift take their coffee break. Outside, cars toot their horns because children have been dropped off at daycare and there are files waiting on desks.

Do you hear it too?

The jazz of aggressive traffic.

This place isn't technically in the city. It's a suburb, with no cinemas, pubs or shopping centres. But it is far from quiet – I hear literally everything.

The accelerating brakes of the cars.

The unashamed tk, tk, tk of high heels that haven't seen the cobbler in a long time.

When it rains, people park themselves underneath the awning above the entrance to the building. Umbrellas are shaken like feathers, sleeves are smoothed out, it's a whole ballet. They – the people, the passers-by – all wait until it gets better. I try to see something of myself in these people when I watch them, but

I see nothing concrete, only small hints and other fleeting things. Insignificant things, like an earring or a hair pin that I also have at home.

In front of the door is a three-lane highway with a bike path in the shade beside it. The asphalt is still so fresh that I can practically hear it crackling. Someone died here a year ago. There was an accident, something to do with a lorry and a cargo bike, which was attributed to the poor state of the road, or, in other words, it was the local council's fault. After that, everything around here has been renovated under the guise of 'city rehabilitation'.

Also fear the green that isn't yet ripe.

The little figures on the traffic lights wear skirts. The length of the skirts betrays an era that wasn't quite as inclusive.

On the opposite side of the highway is a nail salon with bullet holes in the window.

In the slipstream of the morning bike traffic, I see girls on their way to school, wearing the kind of eyeliner that makes them look like victims. I associate them as much with the long-armed goddesses of the past as with modern-day emergency services. They are beautiful girls, the kind whose farts smell like popcorn.

All the chairs here are plastic, everything here is plastic and spherical, child-friendly. All the people who live here have the same level of responsibility as a child. That is to say, nothing is expected of them, they exist and that is enough. In fact, for some of them, their very existence is an amazing feat after the things they have done to themselves.

From my own plastic chair, which I placed beside the window, I watch the day timidly surrender itself. The day is careful and reserved, she never takes any risks – she drives only when she has a green light, and she stops whenever it turns red, never paying any attention to the things that happen in between.

The woman in the stoplight is apparently wearing high heels.

People are on their way to work, to school, to the hospital and once there, they follow the routines that are required of them. In the meantime, I'm wearing tracksuit bottoms and an oversized T-shirt, but I'm absolutely not allowed to go for a run. In fact, I'm not allowed to go anywhere. Stagnation is my only routine.

If I look very closely, I can see lines in the asphalt that are capable of predicting the weather for the coming week. When they (the lines) get it right, a man comes along to reward them with a large water sprayer. In the short time that I've been sitting here, I've seen him twice. He enjoys warning bike riders for the thickness of the hose. The riders that ignore him and attempt to defeat the hose, fall flat on their arses. After which they still have to pick up their bike and manoeuvre their way over the hose. Once they're over the humiliation, their knees will start to sting. It's very warm outside. The streets are thirsty and I'm predicting cloudy skies.

In the bright sunlight, my shadow is perfect. My shadow is the epitome of a human silhouette, a woman's silhouette. She wouldn't look out of place on a toilet door.

There are also bus stops, local supermarkets, bottle banks, and the moral Achilles' heel that they call 'hostile architecture'. Rows of sharp nails under viaducts, on armrests and on ledges and beside the canopied payment machines at parking garages, so there's absolutely no way a homeless person could turn it into a bed.

The day room is located on the top floor, which substantially improves my powers of observation. A luxury apartment building – commonly called the City's Anus, because it is shaped like a sphincter – is my anchor on the horizon. If I start there, I can trace a line to the church that I used to pass every day, but never went into, and the park where I photographed the girl.

And look! These are the buildings that form part of my personal mythology and can't be ignored:

the schoolyard with the ejaculating penis,

my absent Sister's office,

and the vague blue light of the police station.

My lunch is nourishing and practical. I eat it with a plastic spoon, because I wasn't lying when I said that everything here is plastic and spherical, oh no, that's the only kind of thing they trust us – or me – with. It's been thirteen days since I touched anything besides a plastic spoon. I can't even brush my teeth alone. I'm only allowed to shave my armpits if I show good behaviour, something that has yet to happen.

If I ever manage to get out of here, I'm going to get those glow-in-the-dark stars. The chewing gum I'd use as glue would probably reduce the value of my apartment, but it won't stop me, all money is just Monopoly money and anyway, I've never needed to get a mortgage. I could drill a hole in every wall, and I'd still be rich.

Do you want to know what I recently learned?

A plane's black box is actually – fabulists! – orange.

Almost the colour of alarm.

But just a shade lighter, in case the situation ends more fortuitously than anticipated.

My days are monotone and banal, it's true, but I've managed to evade one last tedious thing. I'm walking around gripped by one final fear: that I could die in the same way my father did. A kind of violent and ridiculous death that can't be recounted without scorn, a Looney-Tune death. Quicksand under a clear sky. I tremble waiting for the anvil to fall from the heavens!

The singer my Sister and I both loved listening to turned out to be a paedophile. Yes, it's true, I'm always being targeted by something or someone. But I can handle it – I've seen so many films and the bones I use for sitting are the strongest. I sit and I watch, and my body grows. The longer I'm here, the more my belly fat bulges at the seams of my tracksuit pants. The sheer size of me shows how powerful I am.

I think it's still summer. The days are long but I'm eating as if it's December, at fixed times and in the company of many. Personally, I don't think this is a substitute for a path, order, or a system. Sometimes the day thrusts itself on you like a gag reflex. I wake up, eat something, make logistical resolutions in my plastic chair and – achoo! – the unspeakable arrives.

A billboard above the highway is selling a sunny destination. The holidaymakers either want azure blue water or nothing at all!

Once I was a girl, now I'm a woman. I'm a woman and despite this there are still girls. The difference between us can be measured in cartilage and collagen, self-control, and the ability to put things in perspective. Or rather, experience – and time, lots of it.

I saw an opportunity to dominate time and I took it. Is that so unforgivable?

When you're young it's insulting to be called a child and if, as an adult, you've managed to hold on to the child inside yourself, you'll be labelled inappropriate. The grown-ups will reject you. You weren't responsible enough. You'll become a deserter. You will be humbled.

And the people who don't understand your grief will laugh at your ineptitude, at the things in your drawers, at the birthday of a ghost you've noted in your diary.

Hey, do you see it too?

Televisions, dishwashers, and jeans hanging out of windows.

Days that return every year and bring you something lovely. Petit fours with coffee. Conversations had over glasses of red wine! Keychains.

Am I, Thistle, some higher being's voodoo doll?

From my plastic chair I see the way other people fill their free time. I recognise the outlines of lunchboxes and walking shoes in their bulging backpacks.

I don't mourn it. My time will come.

The future glistens like a useful object.

I'm running towards it – or rather, I'm walking – but this process also takes time, has its conditions, gets interrupted.

The weasels don't visit me anymore. I've banished them from my life, just like my Sister banished the past from hers. We no longer need the past, she and I. We've found something new to fear.

Taxis, viaducts, humiliation.

If I'm ever asked to describe myself in three words, then I'll know I've reached the end of a personality test. I can do anything I want, in spite of what I might write on a form, or which pills I swallow. In my mind, I'm limitless. In my mind, I have tentacles, no deathbed, and two parents. I make music in exchange for money. I pose for the cover of an award-winning album. I'm made slightly immortal under the guise of beauty.

And still, I'm naturally touched by progress. Something changes in my organs. I require more sleep on weeknights. I subscribe to something that brings me joy.

I'll be receptive. I'll accept every task that comes my way and keep my imagination on a leash.

I'll do whatever the present demands and find peace in it. And live like an animal, without any history or feel for chronological order, only making space for the most pressing needs: food, rest, companionship. Everything else is just the sprinkles on top.

At least, that's how I try to live.

Because can you imagine it, having a beautiful voice!

Being able to sing beautifully and using that to express your deepest emotions without being a burden to strangers.

Blissful, frail, and horny you'll be.

Look, how brilliant and tragic.

All those good, lovely people.

With their bike bells, rain ponchos and eyeliner.

People who jump with abandon in group photos, who 'go for drinks' and are 'activated'.

Tiny, dead, happy people who wouldn't hesitate to trust you with their house keys.

People like young birds in a cityscape, who are still willing to eat from your hand because they haven't learned to fear you.

Two beautiful girls stand before me, but I have only one photo in my hands…

the new
**Menard
press**

Thistle
Nadia de Vries

Translated from the Dutch by Sarah Timmer Harvey
Originally published as *De bakvis* by Pluim (NL) in 2022
This edition was first published in The United Kingdom in October 2024
by The New Menard Press

ISBN 9789083384146
First edition, October 2024

The publisher gratefully acknowledges the support of
the Dutch Foundation for Literature.

N ederlands
letterenfonds
dutch foundation
for literature

Text editing by Fannah Palmer
Cover design by Anna Morrison
Typography by Armée de Verre Bookdesign, Ghent, Belgium
Typeset in Joanna Nova by Eric Gill and Ben Jones
Printed by CPI Limited, UK
Distribution and Sales: Booksource, Glasgow (orders@booksource.net)
InPress Ltd Newcastle upon Tyne
www.inpressbooks.co.uk

www.thenewmenardpress.com